Touched by Love

a novel by
Anne Freedman

**Macro
Publishing
Group**

Lansing, Illinois

ISBN: 0-9754130-4-X

Edited by Susan Mary Malone, Christine Meister
and Lissa Woodson
Cover concept by Lissa Woodson
Cover design by Melissa Evangelista

ACKNOWLEDGEMENTS

This book is the result of many who have been an encouragement and support to me. First, I want to pay tribute to my Creator/Redeemer whose love has touched my life; to my parents who always stood by me and nurtured me in unconditional love; to Errol, Chris, Leahan and Tim—true gifts from God who grace my journey though life.

Many thanks also to Lissa Woodson of Macro Publishing Group, a kindly nudge and lady of great strength and vision; to my editors Susan Malone and Christine Meister for their advice and expertise; to Krissy Stenberg, cosmetologist exceptional; to Pete Stenberg, photographer extraordinaire; to Leticia Caldas, the woman with a gorgeous pair of hands; and to Melanie Evangelista for her wonderful cover design.

And finally, to you, dear Reader, who provides me with purpose to weave words into a storyline. The shuttle now grows silent and the invitation beckons: sit back, get comfortable, and let the story unfold!

--*Anne Freedman*
April 7, 2004

Prologue

"No." All eyes turned toward him. He searched their faces for signs of hope, but their straight-lined expressions and saddened eyes only confirmed her words.

"Noooooooo," he cried, running toward the front door without his coat. He burst into the frigid darkness, the anguish of his soul exploding into the stillness of the night. "Nooooooo!!!!!"

She listened, all her senses attuned to the moment – her very being ached with him – their cries joining in time and space. Nothing had prepared them for this. *Oh God, how could this be happening?*

An urgency stirs within me –
How quickly does life grow and bloom.
Choices/consequences intermingle –
Life's petals compressed into perfume.

CƆ Chapter 1 ᏰᎧ

Tasia closed her eyes, attempting to shut out the pain. Her Saturdays were normally filled with grocery shopping, housework, and miscellaneous errands. Today, however, would be different. Today was just for her. Anastasia Franklin, or "Tasia," as she was known, rarely allowed herself that luxury. No, this time was not a *luxury*, but a necessity. Everything was getting so complicated.

Tasia started the day by sleeping in late. When she finally rolled out of bed, she fixed herself a bubble bath, rolled her brown, shoulder-length hair into a makeshift bun, and laid her slender body against the tub, letting the bubbly blanket envelope her.

Thoughts of family began to fill her mind, followed by a barrage of emotions: pain, love, loneliness, sadness, confusion. Her throat constricted against the choking memories. She needed time to sort through it all. Today would be a day of reflection, a time to get centered. She was aware that as she opened the doors to past memories, she would not be alone.

After draining the tub and drying her clean, generously tanned skin, Tasia put on a light blue shirt and denim shorts. She slowly walked down to the kitchen to start a pot of coffee. She felt comforted in her surroundings. The house had an air of peace about it, which was why she had bought it in the first place.

Tasia's and her daughter's bedrooms, along with a full bath, were on the third, upper-most floor. The kitchen and living room filled the mid section. A carpeted room and half-bath made up the first level, which her son had converted into his living quarters. The attached two-car garage was large enough to accommodate her blackish-blue, mid-size Saturn and her son's bright red Mustang.

While the coffee brewed, Tasia pulled back the heavy sliding glass door to the wooden deck and sat down on one of the patio chairs.

How peacefully the creek's murky waters flowed, gently coaxed along by the winding stream's current. *Like the twists and turns of life.* Just past her property, an emerald green cornfield sparkled in the bright sunlight. Her eyes took in the still waters, the green pastures – she could feel her soul being restored.

She closed her eyes and inhaled deeply. *Ah, the fresh smell of the earth.* Tasia felt so at peace here, unlike the turbulent circumstances that had brought her here – a whirlwind that had so altered the course of her life, tearing away the familiar and forcing her to start anew.

Moving had been a necessity. The northwest suburbs of Chicago were a logical choice. Out of all the possibilities, this particular piece of real estate in Elgin was absolutely where she belonged.

The journey that led her here, like the winding creek before her eyes, had taken so many twists and turns. Sometimes life's current had been overpowering. Looking back now, Tasia could see God's faithfulness throughout her journey, even in the midst of the storms.

A soft breeze blew a curly strand of hair across her slender nose, tickling it. Absentmindedly, Tasia pushed the disobedient strand aside, tucking it securely behind her left ear. Occasional glimpses of sunlight peeked through the billowy white clouds overhead. The early afternoon air was quickly warming.

The t-shirt and shorts had been a good selection for today. One never quite knew what the late-August weather would bring. Such days in the Midwest could be summer-time hot or fall-time cool. She preferred it somewhere in between.

About fifty feet of freshly mowed green grass lay between her and the creek. In the distance, a grove of oak trees stood behind the mature cornfield, camouflaging signs of the ever-encroaching, inevitable advance of civilization. She had learned to appreciate the beauty of the present moments in life, and her senses drank it in.

The coffee should be done by now.

As she strolled into the kitchen, she inhaled the nutty aroma of freshly brewed coffee. Sunlight streamed through the skylight in the adjacent living room, banishing any lingering shadows. That was what today was about – *no more shadows!*

Tasia opened the cupboard door just above her head, selected a coffee mug, and smiled. "I love my Mommy" was written across the cup in bright blue scrolled lettering, a present to her from earlier years – one of her favorites.

She poured the hot beverage into the cup and walked back out onto the deck. The sturdy dark green table and four matching chairs were part of the patio set her parents gave as a housewarming gift. She sat down, smiling at their thoughtfulness.

Tasia took a deep breath, the fragrance confirming the satisfying taste as she took a sip of coffee and felt the warm liquid slide down her throat. That first sip of coffee always tasted so good!

The moment had come – no more delays. Tasia took a deep breath and let it out in a soft sigh as she let her thoughts begin to wander.

We're all travelers
Along life's highway and so –
When you come to the fork
Which way will you go?

CHAPTER 2 ❧

Her beloved Ernie was thirty when they met, though at first he had lied about his age. He could have gotten away with it, though. His thick black hair showed no signs of receding, and no age lines had yet drawn themselves across his face. His ruddy coloring made a lovely counterpoint to her slightly olive-toned skin. Their contrasting personalities also complemented each other. He was more subdued; she, more outgoing. Intellectually, he was her equal. Yet, as time would show, they were different in so many ways.

It had been an unusually hot summer, and that particular afternoon was no exception. Tasia's dad had just finished troweling freshly poured concrete by the curb in one of his ongoing home repair projects. A floor tiler by trade, out of necessity he had become quite adept in the Mr. Fix-it role that went along with home ownership.

Ernie parked along the curb in front of the Georgian–style house. Yellow awnings covered the front porch and windows, complementing the blond bricks. The small, modest home was typical of the many homes built during World War II, when building materials were in short supply.

Stepping out of his prized blue 1965 Chevy Impala convertible, Ernie took a final drag on his cigarette, tossed it aside, and snuffed it out with his shoe. He sauntered around the car and onto the service walk alongside the curb. He didn't get very far. Ernie stepped right into the freshly laid concrete before Tasia's dad could get out a word of warning. She smiled. How apologetic Ernie was at the *impression* he made!

That was really getting off on the right foot!

Her mom answered the door before Tasia had a chance to run down the steps. "You must be Ernie Franklin. I'm Tasia's mom.

Come in."

"Nice to meet you, Mrs. Sevalis," Ernie politely replied, stepping through the door.

"And where are you planning on taking my daughter?" she asked.

"I thought we'd go watch the stock car races at Santa Fe Speedway," Ernie replied.

Tasia finished her descent down the stairs. She smiled at him as she walked toward the gap between her mom and Ernie.

He returned the smile. "Hi, Tasia, I'm Ernie. Nice to meet you," he said, looking first at Tasia and then back at her mom. "Ready to go?"

"Hi, Ernie. Yep, ready when you are," she said. His face was closely shaven, his raven black hair cut short. Well, he looked decent enough.

"All right," Tasia's mom replied, glancing over toward Tasia. Her lips were set in a grim line. "Just remember to be home by 11 o'clock."

"Yes, Ma'am," he replied, moving toward the screen door. As he opened it, he titled his head toward Tasia for her to go first.

"See you later, Mom," she said, briskly walking past him. Tasia walked alongside Ernie toward his car.

"Remember to step around," her dad called as he re-trowelled the cement, smoothing away the evidence of Ernie's footstep.

Tasia had never been on a blind date before and had reservations about this one. However, going to the stock car races would be fun, even if her date didn't prove to be.

The roar of the engines as cars jockeyed for position made conversation nearly impossible. Ernie was particularly quiet. Tasia had carried on more conversations with her dog, for heaven's sake!

The ride back home had seemed especially quiet after all the noise of the evening. Well, at least the races were fun. She watched him from the side of her eye as he drove, the wheels against the road the only sound. Tasia sighed with relief when he finally pulled up to her house.

Ernie turned, facing Tasia. His thick black eyebrows bent, as if in pain. "Can I see you again? Lucy and Mel are going up to Fox Lake tomorrow morning. Thought maybe we could double date with them,"

Ernie suggested, his dark brown eyes widened slightly as he turned off the ignition.

"Sure, why not?" Tasia responded, shrugging as she reached for her purse. That was the most he'd spoken nearly all night.

"Good – pick you up at 10?" He looked at her full-faced.

Tasia nodded, turning and groping for the door handle. She walked briskly toward her house, the roar of the engine fading as Ernie drove away.

Sure, why not see him again? At least, it would get her out of the house.

Funny, most people she knew looked forward to the comforts of their home and family. But for her, home was a hotbed of emotions – anger and frustration, mostly. The less time spent there, the better. Besides, the next day she and Ernie would double date with their mutual friends at the beach. At least she would have fun with them, even if she couldn't get Ernie to talk.

The next day, Ernie opened up and apologized for last night's dud of a date. He explained that despite how sick he had felt – he'd had sunstroke – he wasn't one to go back on his word, even if it meant keeping a *blind* date. Tasia admired that – at least the part about keeping his word.

At Fox Lake they set up a picnic table under some shade trees, while Lucy and Mel set up their blanket about ten yards away on the sunny beach. Obviously, they wanted to be alone. Ernie took off his shirt and Tasia saw his blistery, lobster–red skin. She was surprised to find herself feeling sorry for him. Lucy and Mel were soon off playing in the water, splashing and laughing.

"Go ahead and join them, if you want," Ernie said, offering her a Salem. "But there's *no way* I'm leaving the shade today."

"Nah, think I'll just stay here and enjoy the breeze." Tasia leaned over to let Ernie light her cigarette. She inhaled briefly and then turned her head to exhale, softly blowing the smoke out between her lips. "So tell me, how'd you manage to get sunstroke anyway?"

"You probably won't believe this, but here goes. I was out on the balcony at my apartment last Sunday afternoon. It was cloudy, so I didn't think it would matter how long I stayed out. Wound up falling asleep and woke up four hours later, toasted!" He laughed. "Didn't know you could get so sunburned on a cloudy day."

"Yeah, I've found that out the hard way, too," Tasia said, her ponytail sliding across her left shoulder as she tilted her head to one side, nodding.

"But that wasn't the worst of it. The next day I woke up with blisters and couldn't even get dressed for work. Had to take the week off. The first few days, the only way I could even get around was by crawling on my hands and knees!"

Tasia grimaced.

"Today's actually the first day I feel halfway decent. Still felt kind of queasy yesterday – guess I wasn't much fun as a date!" Both he and Tasia laughed. Ernie and Tasia talked and laughed until the sun set. This time the drive home flew by.

"I had a great time, Ernie," Tasia said, wiping the perspiration off her forehead as they pulled alongside the curb.

"Me, too," Ernie said. His pants legs stuck to his sunburned skin. He winced as he turned to face her. "When can I see you again, Tasia?"

"Well, I'm busy next Saturday. How 'bout Sunday afternoon?" Tasia was now fully turned toward Ernie. In truth, she *was* busy. She had another date lined up, but Ernie didn't need to know that.

They set the time and place.

Pausing slightly, he leaned toward her just a bit and hesitated.

Such kind eyes. She leaned toward him. A gentle kiss passed between them. Just a light touching of lips, really, yet enough that there was no mistake. They would meet again.

A chilly breeze jolted Tasia out of the past. Her coffee was ice cold and she felt goose bumps rise on her arms from the cool breeze. My, it's getting cold out!" she exclaimed. Pale pink and crimson hues began to highlight the sea of clouds stretching out toward the horizon. How long had she been sitting here?

The years have passed –
She's a woman now;
Erect with head lifted high
And every right to be proud.

Cʒ CHAPTER 3 ᛒ

Dinnertime had changed so over the course of years. Meals had become simpler affairs, as it was now just the three of them. They had been through many transitions, with the expectation of more to come. Tonight, however, she would make something a little special – perhaps spaghetti and meatballs, with garlic bread on the side.

After being home for the summer, Lizzie was preparing to go back to Michigan for her senior year at Winona State University. Tasia never looked forward to her daughter's departures. No matter how she would like time to stand still, Lizzie's leaving in a couple of weeks was inevitable.

They could have won one of those mother-daughter look-alike competitions. At exactly five feet, Lizzie was somewhat shorter than her mother, but had Tasia's curly dark brown hair, delicate facial characteristics, and mannerisms. Many times Tasia's mother had commented on the genuine love and respect they had for each other.

It had also been that way with Josh and Ernie. Josh was Tasia's first-born – the son of their delight. My, how he resembled his father! Now fully grown, he'd inherited Ernie's black hair, dark brown eyes, ruddy complexion and deep voice. In stature, they were nearly equal in height – five feet, seven inches. Josh also had developed Ernie's quick wit and dry sense of humor, although Josh tended to be more on the social side than his father. Also like his father, he had opted for the trades, but chose the heating and air-conditioning field.

And laugh! My how Lizzie and Josh could laugh! As a child,

Josh knew just how to aggravate his sister almost to the point of tears. As the ever-dutiful parent, Tasia would move in to break it up and then the next thing she knew, Josh and Lizzie would turn it into a comedy fest.

Tasia glanced at the clock as the front door creaked open.

"Hi, Mom," Josh said, using the toe of one foot to push the gym shoe off his other foot. With off-white carpeting throughout the house, shoe removal was expected. "Mmmm, smells good in here."

"Spaghetti! Wow—didn't realize how hungry I was till just now," exclaimed Lizzie, quickly tossing her shoes into the closet.

"Hi, guys – you're just in time. Dinner's nearly ready." Tasia held up a cooling spoonful of the homemade spaghetti sauce for a last-minute taste test. "How'd it go?"

Josh and Lizzie walked into the kitchen to greet her. "Fine," Josh said. "Met up with some friends from the old neighborhood and took Lizzie for a ride past our old house. You remember Tony, Yong, Mike and Chrissy?" He reached into the pot of strained spaghetti and snatched one. "Hmm, just right."

"I sure do," Tasia said as she laid the spoon on the counter. "How are they doing?"

"They're fine. Send you their regards. Boy, you should see what the new people have done to the place!"

"Really? Like what?" Tasia asked, smiling at both of them and thankful for their close bond.

"Well, for starters, the basketball hoop is down from the garage," Josh said, looking toward Lizzie.

"Well, guess we know *that* would've made an impact on you," Tasia replied, smiling.

Lizzie's hazel green eyes lit up as she added, "The big blue spruce and large evergreen trees are gone from in front of the house, too." She dried her petite hands on the kitchen towel hanging from the oven's handle. "And they put a fence up around the yard."

"Guess it must look really different." Tasia spooned long strands of noodles into a heap on each of their plates.

"Yeah, and strange," Lizzie added, shrugging.

"Well, let's get this food going." Tasia topped each mound of noodles with a ladleful of sauce. "Lizzie, you want to help me put this out on the table? Josh, you pour the milk. I'll get the garlic bread out of the toaster oven, and then we'll be ready."

They sat around the oval oak table in the kitchenette that served as both kitchen and dining room. The aroma of garlic permeated the house.

"I was thinking," Tasia started while twirling her fork in the steaming noodles, "maybe next weekend we could go visit Grandma. I know she'd love to see you guys."

Both agreed.

"All right, then," Tasia said. "After dinner I'll give Grandma a call."

When dinner was done, Tasia dialed her mom's telephone number, while Josh and Lizzie cleared the table and washed the dishes.

"Yeah, it was beautiful out today." Tasia grabbed one of the blue throw pillows she had made years earlier and positioned it against the corner of the couch to lean against. "I actually got a chance to enjoy it for a change. Say, Mom, will you be home next weekend? The kids and I were thinking of taking a ride out to see you before Lizzie has to go back."

They made plans. Josh and Lizzie joined Tasia in the living room. "Grandma says she's looking forward to seeing us next weekend. Seemed to perk right up when she heard we were all coming," she said. She rearranged her pillow to make room for Lizzie who sank into the middle of the sagging couch cushion next to her.

"Mom, there's something I want to talk to you about." Josh reached for the remote control and lowered the volume.

"Well, you've certainly got my undivided attention. What it is, Josh?" Tasia turned to face him.

"I've been checking out different apartments and think I found a place. Bob and I can split the rent, and it's not too far from work." Josh's honey-brown eyes lit up with excitement as he described the place to Tasia. "The only drawback is that there's no garage. But if it's okay with you, I'd like to leave my workbench and tools here until I get better situated."

"So, you're planning on leaving me, too?" Tasia tried to keep a straight face, but when she saw the concern on Josh's face, she couldn't pull it off and broke into a smile. "Actually, that's great, Josh. In fact, if your dad were still with us, no doubt you'd have been out long ago."

The room became quiet. Lizzie cleared her throat. "Hey, bro, maybe tomorrow you can take me over to see it."

"Yeah, you can give me your feedback." Josh got up and walked toward the kitchen, stopping in front of Tasia. "You all right, Mom?"

"Sure, Josh, why'd ya ask?" She looked into her son's clear brown eyes and could see the jumble of emotions swimming around in them.

"Oh, nothing…just checking, that's all." He continued on his way, poured a glass of apple cider and returned to the living room to join them on the couch.

After watching the evening news, Tasia kissed them both goodnight and headed toward the stairs. "See you guys in the morning. Sweet dreams, you two. I love you."

"Love you, too, Mom," Josh replied, not taking his gaze off the screen.

"Me, too," Lizzie chimed in, looking up. "Can't believe in a couple more weeks, I'll be headed back up."

"Yeah," Tasia said. *More transitions.*

Resting on her bed, she stared blankly at the white ceiling overhead. Being all together again was so good.

The decision is yours,
You alone must decide –
Which way will you choose?
Will you accept or deny?

☪ Chapter 4 ☪

She awoke to birds singing and chirping relentlessly outside her bedroom window. Slowly opening her left eye, she peered at the sun's rays streaming through the lace curtains. What time was it, anyway? She turned and slowly focused on the digital display of her clock radio. Eight o'clock? "Time to get your lazy butt out of bed, girl!"

Tasia rolled out of bed and got ready. Eight-thirty. Kurt should be here any minute. She bounced down the stairs and prepared a pot of coffee. He said he wanted to sit in on her Sunday School class with the third-through-fifth graders this morning. She wasn't sure how they'd react to his presence, but being a former fifth-grade teacher himself, she wasn't too worried. As Tasia reached for a cup, she heard a soft knock on the front door.

"Good morning, Kurt. C'mon in." Tasia closed the door behind him.

"Top o' the mornin' to ye, lassie," he teased, his bright blue eyes dancing. "Didn't want to wake the kids in case they were still sleeping." He caught the aroma of freshly brewed coffee wafting down the stairway. "Say, have we got time for a cup of cava before we go?"

"Sure. It'll give us a chance to go over the lesson together. As long as we're there by 9, we're good."

The class went great. Kurt's presence didn't seem to stifle the class; if anything, it enhanced it. Tasia enjoyed the stimulating questions the children raised. After class was over, she and Kurt joined the rest of the congregation for the church service. She'd been attending Elgin Vineyard for about a year and enjoyed Pastor Tom's preaching and the close fellowship of other believers.

As the music started playing, Tasia and Kurt joined their voices with the melody and other worshipers in praise. Tasia loved the deep tones emitted from Kurt's barrel chest as his voice blended with hers. As they sang 'How Great Thou Art,' Kurt put his arm around Tasia's waist. Whether caused by reverberating currents of sound or something else, waves of electricity gently flowed through her. Never before had Tasia experienced such a spiritually climactic sensation with another person. The pastor's sermon was about the importance of forgiveness. After the service was over, some friends stopped to chat with them on their way out. Tasia liked these people and her life experiences thus far had equipped her with insights to help encourage some of them in their own particular trials. Sometimes, however, she was the one in need of comfort and advice. That was, after all, how the church was meant to function.

After church, they stopped for lunch at Denny's in Spring Hill Mall. The food was generally good for the price and they could usually count on being seated quickly.

Kurt reached over the table and took hold of Tasia's hand resting on the table's edge. "You know what I'd love to do this afternoon?"

Tasia looked into his twinkling blue eyes – those eyes so full of life. "Don't have a clue, except that it's such a gorgeous day, I'm hoping it has something to do with the great outdoors."

"Well, that's part of it. What'd ya say if after we're done eating, we get changed and go for a bike ride along the river?" The Fox River ran through the heart of Elgin, dividing it into east and west sections. A reclamation effort was underway to beautify the remaining natural parcels of land along its banks. The bike path extended for miles upon miles in either direction.

"Oh, Kurt, that's a great idea. Lizzie is going with Josh to explore apartments this afternoon, and they won't be home till late anyway."

They couldn't have picked a better day for a bike ride. The sun was high in the sky, but not warm enough to cause them to sweat as they peddled past marshes of tall cattails and varieties of wild grass. Birds flitted back and forth in the branches overhead, as the river rolled lazily alongside the path. They stopped in a grassy clearing for a short break.

Tasia rested her bike alongside a tree stump, reached for her water bottle, and took several short gulps. The clear cool liquid moistened her dry mouth and throat. "Ah, that is so good!"

Kurt chugged a few gulps himself. "Yep, sure is refreshing all the way around." He looked at her, his lips turned upward in a boyish grin. "Tasia," he began, singing her name, "I can't imagine life without you. You know much I love you." He put his water bottle back in its slot and took a few steps toward her, pulling her close to him. His kiss was gentle and sweet. "Do you have an answer for me yet, m' lady?"

Tasia pulled her head back, allowing his embrace to hold her against his chest. She looked into his expectant blue eyes, her own wide open, imploring. "Oh, Kurt, I love you, too. But I can't rush into this. There's so much to consider. Most of all, I have to be sure this is what God wants for me…for us." She rested her head on his shoulder as he gently stroked her long hair.

"Then I'll just have to keep on asking and waiting until you get your answer."

Sorrow lasts but for a season,
Seasonal clouds do cry –
Preparing the ground for changes
And tears that eventually dry.

CB CHAPTER 5 BO

Early on, her parents' marriage had been stormy. Theirs was a mixed marriage, not of race but of ancestral nationalities. Her father's family bloodlines were Greek; her mother's, Italian and German. Tasia's mother had never felt good enough or accepted by her in-laws. After all, she had different customs, couldn't cook their dishes, and looked different. She'd always felt like an outsider. Marriage only accentuated that and drove the wedge deeper.

Her parents eventually made their home in Midtown, an Italian neighborhood on Chicago's west side. In the midst of raising four children and struggling to pay bills, they made educating their children in the local parish school a priority.

Tasia's family lived as most lower-middle income people do – surviving day-to-day. Her father, an honest hard worker, had his own floor-tiling business. But after materials were purchased and laborers were paid, not much was left for the fledgling family.

As soon as the children were old enough, her mother joined the workforce. Tasia was in charge of her two younger brothers, Joey and Tom. Her older brother, Ken, was probably glad he wasn't one of the younger brothers, as Tasia kept a close eye on them. He considered Tasia a nuisance, something she supposed was typical for an older brother. But in her case, it was even more so because of the turbulence he said she caused constantly within the family.

Not that her parents didn't love her. They did.

Trying to be "good" hadn't worked with Tasia, so what was the sense of trying? She had never been able to please her mother. The more her mother would push, the more Tasia would push right back. Like two bulls bucking horns, neither one backed down. Verbal and physical assaults had forged Tasia into the headstrong, defiant person she had become.

Things hadn't always been that way. Tasia's earliest memory was that of being a young girl, perhaps around three or four years of age, helping her mother wash the dining room floor on her hands and knees, as was her mother's custom. Even then, Tasia knew something was different between the way her mother treated her and her older brother Ken.

That afternoon, Tasia asked her mother why she didn't love her. The only part of her mother's response that she remembered was, "Because you look like your father's side of the family." Though Tasia didn't fully comprehend the meaning of the response then, it cut deeply into her soul.

And so, Tasia became the brunt of her mother's frustration. Tasia's strong spirit sustained her through those tumultuous childhood years, even though her strong spirit and body were bruised and battered along the way.

Tasia was no longer that little girl who cried herself to sleep at night, asking God to make her nicer so that her mother would love her.

Did God even love her? Tasia's concept of God was that of a stern judge who didn't have time to be bothered with her requests. That must be why everyone in her religion prayed to Mary and the saints. Besides, if God really did care about Tasia, why didn't He care about what was happening in her life? She saw no way out of it. She would just have to tough it out until she could eventually make it on her own.

The parochial grammar school established a strict environment where education was taken very seriously. Tasia felt safe there and knew what was expected of her. The nuns took an interest in her and she worked hard to please them. For a while, she fed on her teachers' encouragement and support. As Tasia grew older, that just wasn't enough.

Around the age of ten, one of Tasia's classmates began teaching the awkward-looking adolescent the piano. Drawing a keyboard on a length of cardboard, Tasia would practice her fingering of the scales.

Noticing her interest, her parents bought a miniature electronic keyboard for her to learn on. When she went as far as she could on that, one Christmas Tasia's father bought her a full-sized piano. Tasia knew the tremendous sacrifice her parents had made to purchase that piano and was determined to play it well.

That piano became a haven for her. How had she missed God's hand in that?

After several years of lessons, practicing, and participating in recitals, her instructor suggested Tasia continue training at a music conservatory. But her parents just didn't have that kind of money. And so she closed that door reluctantly, but with finality.

Grades came easily to Tasia, who now turned her energies elsewhere.

Even though still young, she carried the weight of responsibility as if she were much older. At fifteen, she got her first job at a Burger King about a half-mile away from home. Although it only paid minimum wage, that job opened up the world to her —a world that could be exciting, but also scary, especially on those long walks home from work by herself late at night.

Tasia never considered college as an option because of her folks' financial constraints. After all, they still had three sons to get through school. So after her sophomore year of high school, Tasia, her friend Lucy, and some other classmates transferred to Jones Commercial High School where she completed her junior and senior years. One of the school's requirements was to work part-time in a business environment that coincided with the student's selected major.

At the time, people were protesting the U.S.'s involvement in the Vietnam War. Tasia organized her own little protest over certain school policies at Jones that she and others believed to be unfair. Armed with protest signs, she and about twenty of her friends and fellow students picketed in front of the school gate.

The school, however, did not tolerate such behavior and promptly called a paddy wagon to haul the disruptive students off to jail. In disbelief, Tasia watched as several of her peers were placed in the back of the paddy wagon and whisked away. She, along with the others under eighteen, were promptly escorted to the principal's office and suspended.

However, the protest ultimately proved to be effective. In the few weeks remaining before graduation, Tasia headed the newly formed, first-time-ever student council. The council passed several measures modifying outdated school policies. But even that had come at a price. Her name and picture were removed from the yearbook before publication – the administration's final retribution.

An analyzer, never content with shallow explanations or surface living, Tasia was all too well aware of the complexities and entanglements of life.

In her senior year, Tasia was already employed full-time at Shapiro & Kahn, a small two-man law firm in downtown Chicago, living paycheck to paycheck, as did most folks she knew. The busy work environment provided Tasia with valuable experience. She ran nearly everything in that office and enjoyed the busy pace of being receptionist, stenographer, typist, bookkeeper, and paralegal, all rolled up into one. She was getting good experience and her bosses were getting a good deal.

Looking back, Tasia was amazed to even be alive. "Something" had prevented her from showing up the night she was supposed to be initiated into a girls' street gang. That night, a rival gang had taken out their vengeance on the group and some of the girls had been killed. If Tasia had been there.... God's hand was already guiding her steps, in spite of herself.

A few months after that incident, her heart had been crushed when a boyfriend broke up with her. Years later, Tasia would find out he had been killed on a street corner in a drug bust. Another detour of God's grace.

God's hand was all over Tasia's life, to be sure. Just how little did she realize it at the time!

Your presence surrounds me – I'm covered in love!
Now a man You have brought to my side.
What are these stirrings that so thrill my soul?
Tingling sensations of love's butterflies.

CƷ Chapter 6 ꝯ

Unlike Tasia, whose tendency was to openly show her emotions, Ernie wasn't much for outward displays of affection—not even holding hands. Tasia tried to understand that side of him. He must have been hurt deeply to close off that part of himself. Ernie was a practical sort of a guy – not a head-in-the-clouds, mushy-gushy type of person.

Tasia knew that the bitterness of a failed marriage still gnawed within him, compounding his pain. The heat of their fights and his ex-wife's unfaithfulness had formed a hard shell coating Ernie's heart. Could he ever trust again?

Not even their young son, Pete, had escaped unscathed. Barbara's hot anger found its release venting on those around her. That whole marriage had been a mistake, and Barbara was left with an inconvenient reminder – their son. Witchcraft and drugs offered an appealing escape for her. It became easy to rationalize her responsibilities away, leaving Pete in the more capable care of the only two women she still trusted. After all, her mother and grandmother were more experienced in childrearing, anyway.

Whenever Ernie would get into the car to pick up Pete, he never knew where he'd find his son. He often wound up driving futilely from one place to another until he located the dark-haired little boy.

"It's a good thing those women all live close to each other," he had told Tasia one day, after a particularly trying attempt to pick up his son.

Pete had fine facial features like his mother, but Ernie's jet-black hair, which always looked in need of a trim. He was just a little guy for a four-year-old. His arms and legs were rather thin in comparison to other children his age, but his little tummy stuck out enough to make Tasia think he was at least being fed properly. As she spent more time with Pete, Tasia realized he was a smart little boy, verbally advanced for his young age. But he lacked social contact with his peers, except for some limited interaction in kindergarten. Much to Ernie's dismay, Pete's great-grandmother had decided that in their racially changing neighborhood, he would be safer if kept indoors.

After a two-year stormy marriage, Ernie was served with divorce papers. He joined the ranks of other weekend dads, left to sort out the remaining pieces of his life.

Tasia's attraction to Ernie continued to grow with each encounter. By autumn, they started dating exclusively. Ernie wasn't one to chit-chat just to kill time. He was comfortable with quietness – maybe a little too comfortable. Although he was not comfortable with physical displays of affection, a fact that disturbed Tasia, their relationship was growing steadily. She felt secure when she was with Ernie, a feeling she hadn't experienced dating other guys.

Tasia considered herself to be an attractive enough gal – a bit heavy on the make-up, though. Her curly, dark brown hair draped like a veil over her shoulders. At five feet, five inches, she found it slightly comforting to be an inch or so shorter than Ernie. Funny how society impacted one's expectations.

As summer sped away with autumn nipping at its heels, Tasia was left with pleasant memories of the warm sun tanning her skin and picnics spent together at the lake. With so much to learn about each other, there just never seemed to be enough time.

"Tasia, you're too young to be getting so seriously involved with a man," her mother said one night at the dinner table. Her voice took on its characteristic sharp edge. "Not that your father and I totally disapprove of him as a person, but after all, he does have the stigma of being divorced, as well as the responsibilities of raising a young son."

"You haven't given him a *chance*," Tasia countered, forcing down a mouthful of food as her stomach tightened. "He's a good man. I wish you and Dad would at least *try* to get to know him." Tasia looked directly into her mother's steely gray eyes, not backing down.

Their loud, agitated voices filled the house. Home was not a peaceful place when Tasia was around.

Life became a blur. The only peace Tasia knew was with Ernie. She felt safe and secure with him, but always had to return to the turmoil of home.

Shortly after Thanksgiving Day, Ernie proposed. Tasia accepted, knowing full well that the battle line with her parents was now clearly drawn – a scenario that would have to be played out, whether she liked it or not.

Arriving home past her assigned curfew on that special date night, Tasia announced her engagement to her mother.

"Tasia, do you realize what time it is?" Her mother stood in the doorway in her cotton robe, hands on hips, frowning. "How dare you defy my wishes again!"

"Mom, there's something you need to know," Tasia said, following her into the dining room. When her mother pivoted to confront Tasia further, Tasia held out her left hand, displaying the simple silver band with its sparkling round diamond on her fourth finger.

"Tasia...No! No! I won't have it! You give it back to him!"

"No, Mom," Tasia said. She returned her mother's glare unwaveringly, every cell in her body in stress mode. "We love each other."

Her father walked sleepily into the dining room in his pajamas, his slippers brushing against the floor with each step, to find out what was causing all the commotion. Tasia showed him her engagement ring, searching his round face for signs of a reaction.

His dark eyes widened as he wiped the sleep from his eyelids. "Tasia, are you sure this is what you want?"

"Yes, Dad." She so wanted his approval, but was prepared not to get it.

"Then, God's blessings to you both," he said, holding his arms open wide.

Tasia hugged him gratefully, her eyes welling with tears.

"Is that all you have to say to her?" her mother demanded, looking at her husband with thin eyebrows raised at high mast and mouth open wide.

"What's done is done." Raising both arms emphatically, he looked into his wife's stunned face. "I'm going back to bed and suggest you do the same." He took a step and then hesitated, waiting for her to join him.

Tasia's mom, however, stood firm. Her father turned and slowly walked away. More angry words were exchanged until finally, Tasia was shown the door.

By mutual agreement, she left home that night, walking defiantly out the living room door as it closed with a quiet thud behind her. At eighteen, Tasia was on her own.

She rebounded quickly and spent that night and the next at her girlfriend's house. While there, she heard about a basement apartment for rent a bit closer to downtown. It wasn't much, but Tasia didn't need much, and the price was right.

The two-room furnished apartment had been converted from some spare space in Mrs. Delanova's basement. For $65.00 a month, Tasia now had a place of her own with a bed, stove, refrigerator, and shower.

That weekend, Tasia called home.

"Tasia, how are you? We've been so worried!" her mother asked.

"I'm fine, Mom. No need to worry," Tasia replied, her eyebrows raising at her mother's caring interest. "Found a little apartment to live in."

"Oh? Where?"

Tasia could hear the heavy dining room chair scraping against the linoleum floor on the other end of the phone. "A few miles east of you on 63rd Street."

"How much is the rent? Who *else* is living with you?"

"Sixty-five dollars a month, and *no one's* living with me, Mom. Not Ernie, or anyone else, for that matter."

Her mom's voice softened back to its original caring tone. "I'd like to come see it and meet the landlord."

Was this a test or was she really being sincere? "Really? Well, okay, Mom. Actually, the reason for my call is I was wondering if I could come by this evening to pick up my clothes. Then, if you still want, I'll bring you over."

"Yes, Tasia, I'd like that," she replied. "I'll see you later then."

Her apartment was near a major intersection, so Tasia could walk to the corner and catch the local bus to get downtown to her job. The landlord was a little nosier than she cared for, but it would do for now.

Quietness replaced commotion. Despite their arguments and quarrels, deep down her mother really cared about her. Her mother just had very definite ideas of what a daughter should be.

Unfortunately, Tasia didn't fit that mold.

The child grew in wisdom and grace,
Learning of this dimension's plights –
Endowed with gifts from her creator –
Strengthened through the trials of life.

CȜ CHAPTER 7 ɮ

Summer vacation was winding down. Tasia spent the last week reviewing the new curriculum and setting up her classroom for another school year. Like an expectant mother, she looked forward to a new batch of third-graders, seeing their faces, expanding their minds, and alerting them to consequences of reckless behavior. These days, there was too much of that going around.

Lizzie had given her notice at the nursing home where she had worked as a recreational therapist during the summer months. One more week and she would be heading back to college.

Josh's work was in its predictable seasonal slowdown as the summer months waned. Then with the first cold snap, it would open full throttle again. He had taken Tasia to see his new 'digs' before signing the lease with Bob. Josh and Bob had been friends since grammar school. Bob was a big guy – could have been a football player – but opted for a career in architecture instead.

Tasia voiced her approval. It was well-maintained, and though the rent was high, it wasn't unreasonable by today's standards. "It's a nice place with easy enough access to the expressway. I'm glad you and Bob will be splitting the rent. Boy, I can't believe how much rents have increased since your dad and I moved out of our apartment in Mt. Prospect, let alone my first apartment." Tasia smiled wryly in remembrance. *You've come a long way, baby, since those early days in that basement apartment!*

Early Sunday afternoon, Tasia, Lizzie, and Josh made the familiar drive to her mom's house. Lizzie was first out of the car; Josh and Tasia followed right behind. Tasia rang the doorbell and waited for her mom to answer. Her mom moved a little more slowly these days. A lot of years had come and gone since Tasia's childhood.

Josh and Lizzie loved their Grandma and vice versa. Thankfully, whatever had transpired between Tasia and her parents years before hadn't affected their relationship with their grandparents, thank God. Yeah, maybe their relatives were a little different, but whose family was perfect?

"Well, well, you made it!" Tasia's mom greeted them enthusiastically and opened the screen door wide. "Come on in and make yourselves at home."

"Hi, Mom. Good to see you," Tasia said with a warm hug, which was just as warmly returned.

"Lizzie, Josh – come on in. There you go," she said, hugging each one. "I just got done making some stew, in case you get hungry later."

"Uh, Mom," Tasia said, "I don't think we'll be staying too long today. Actually, I'd like to be on the road by six."

"Oh, that's fine," Tasia's mom said. A cloud passed over her gray eyes. She blinked it back, just barely masking her disappointment. "Well, if you don't eat any here, you can take some home with you for dinner tonight." Turning back to her grandchildren, she asked, "So, Josh, what have you been up to lately?" Before Josh had a chance to respond, she added, "And Lizzie, I'm so glad you could visit before returning to school."

"Yeah, Gramma, the summer's gone by so fast," Lizzie said, closing the heavy wooden front door securely and facing her again. "But that's three years behind me now."

She sighed. "Well, I just wish I could've been able to help you out."

"That's okay, Gramma," Lizzie responded. She moved toward her grandmother and gently stroked her arm. The thinning flesh rolled and wrinkled under Lizzie's touch. "It'll be all right. I've already got a part-time job lined up for the fall, so that will help me get through it."

"You're as determined as your mother, Lizzie." She chuckled. "And how 'bout you, Josh? What have you been up to lately?"

"Well, for starters, I just co-signed on a lease for an apartment."

Her mouth opened, then broke into a grin. "That's good, Josh.

Glad to see you're getting on with your life. Let's sit down and you can tell me more about it." She took a seat in the recliner, carefully easing her way into its soft, comfortable cushion.

Josh took her cue and sat down across from her on the simple pine-framed couch. "Well, it's about a half-hour drive from work – right near the expressway. My friend Bob's splitting the rent with me, so that'll help out."

"Does it have a garage for your Mustang?"

"No, just a regular parking lot, but that's okay. I've scraped icy windows before." His laughter lit up the room.

She smiled widely. "Yes, guess we all have! And how's your job going?"

Josh shifted his weight on the upholstered foam rubber cushion. "It's good, but we're entering the slow season now. As the weather gets colder, more service calls'll start coming in as everyone will want their furnaces running and humming."

Tasia and Lizzie joined him on the couch.

"Reminds me of your grandfather. His work was pretty seasonal, too…." Her gaze moved over the horizon for a second, but she caught herself and continued, "So, when the money's there, just make sure you save up enough to carry you through the lean times and you'll be fine." She looked over toward Tasia, who nodded.

"So, any boyfriends or girlfriends I should know about?"

Josh and Lizzie both looked at each other and shook their heads. "Nope," Josh replied for both of them.

Tasia walked over to the framed pictures on the bookshelf. She studied the photo of a beautiful young bride dressed in a flowing white satin dress with trailing veil. The groom's face was narrower than she had known, their heads leaning toward each other, smiling lovingly. Her parents had made such a pretty couple. Next to it was a more recent picture of her dad sitting at a piano wearing a big smile on his much rounder face. It was taken at a family gathering for their forty-fifth anniversary. Dad was always happiest when all the family was together. After that picture was taken, his health took a turn for the worse. His death had been sudden and unexpected. It was still hard for her mom to talk about him. Heck, they all missed him. Tasia felt the familiar ache in her heart.

Josh got up and stood next to her. A picture of all the grandchildren posing for a group shot caught his eye. He was the oldest of eleven grandchildren. Tasia knew that he and Lizzie sometimes felt out of place when all the family got together. There was no one else their age. Even Pete was older. *Pete.* She shook her head.

The kids liked the familiarity of their grandmother's home. Not every kid had a grandparent who still lived in the same house where their mom had been raised.

"I just wish you weren't so far away," Tasia's mom said. "Everybody's gone off in their own direction." She looked at them all before continuing, "I guess I just get a little lonely sometimes."

"I know, Mom. *I really do!*" Tasia stepped over toward her mom and patted her bent shoulder. "And come next week, Lizzie'll be 300 miles away until whenever we can get together again. But, that's just part of life. Children need to grow up, leave, and make lives of their own." Now Tasia paused, gazing at her two grown children and sighed. "Life's always changing; *nothing* stays the same. And sometimes…maybe, that's a good thing."

Lizzie walked over to Josh. "Hey, bro, wanna play some catch?"

"Sure, if you think you can handle it."

She laughed, punching him gently on his muscular shoulder. "You know better than that!"

They tromped through the dining room, kitchen, and down the back stairway. The screen door screeched shut. Tasia remembered watching her young son play catch with Ernie during family functions when they 'just needed to get some fresh air.' Yeah, there were lots of good memories for Josh and Lizzie here; there were roots here. Their new house just didn't feel like home to them yet. Would it ever?

"Tasia, are you all right?" her mom asked. "It seems you're off in another world somewhere. I started to tell you something, but I guess you were deep in thought."

"Oh, sorry 'bout that, Mom," Tasia replied, repositioning herself on the couch. "Yeah, guess you could say I've had a lot on my mind lately. What was it you were saying?"

"Just what a nice family you have." She sat down next to Tasia and gave her a warm hug. "I'm so proud of you, Tasia – you and your children."

Tasia was very thankful for their relationship. What a gift God had given her. "Thanks, Mom, you know we love you very much, too. I know it hasn't always been easy for you, either." Tasia took hold of her mother's hands and examined them briefly. Such hard working hands. She enveloped them in her own. "Actually, that's what I've been doing lately – just thinking back, doing a lot of pondering and remembering."

"Anything in particular?"

Tasia adjusted herself on the cushion to face her mother. "Pretty much everything, but it all comes down to God's faithfulness." Still holding her mother's hands, she patted them gently. "And lots of memories…."

"I like to remember the good things, Tasia. And I'm so grateful for the change in you." She cupped Tasia's hands in hers and held them close. "I was always so worried about you, Tasia. You were such a stubborn, headstrong girl that I felt I had to be extra strict with you to keep you in line."

"I know, Mom." Tasia looked into her mom's open face, lined with years of concern. Tasia leaned closer. "Mom, can I ask your opinion about something?"

Her mother smiled. "Can't imagine my opinion would make that much difference, but I'm glad to give it."

Tasia's eyes closed slightly. "No, seriously, Mom. You know that Kurt and I have been dating for a while. What do you think of him – I mean, *really* think of him?"

Her mother's expression mirrored Tasia's. "Well, I think he's a nice man. It concerns me that he's been divorced, although Ernie had been, too. I guess these days it's not all that uncommon anymore. Why do you ask, Tasia?"

Tasia lowered her head, then raised it, her brow furled. "Mom, Kurt's been talking about us getting married."

She studied Tasia's face. "And you said….?"

"I said I couldn't give him an answer just yet. I know it's been several years since Ernie's been gone, but there's still so much to sort out." Tasia rubbed the side of her temple with her hand.

Her mother nodded slowly. "It *is* an important decision, and I can tell you're not taking it lightly. What do Josh and Lizzie think?"

Tasia shook her head. "I haven't mentioned it to them yet. To tell you the truth, I'm not sure what their reactions will be – I'm not even sure of mine at this point."

Her mother got up slowly and moved gingerly toward the windows. "Then it's time to seek a higher intelligence." She turned around and faced her daughter. "God's never let you down yet."

Tasia rose and stood next to her mom. "Yeah, guess that's what it all comes down to."

They spent the rest of the afternoon in light discussion, until it was time to leave.

"Oh, before you go, let me give you some stew to take home with you for supper tonight," Tasia's mom offered. She went into the kitchen and removed a clear plastic container from the cabinet, filling it to the brim with stew. "There, now you're ready," she said as she handed it to Josh.

"Thanks, Gramma," Josh said, following Lizzie's lead into the living room. Tasia and her mom tracked behind them, until the little group assembled once more at the front door.

Tasia hugged and kissed her goodbye, followed in turn by Josh and Lizzie.

Another final hug passed between them. "I love you, Mom."

"I love you, too, Tasia. I'll pray you get the answer you need."

"Goodbye, Gramma," Josh and Lizzie said, as they each got another hug and kiss, then turned and walked out the doorway.

"Goodbye you two. God bless you!" she called out after them from the front porch as they climbed into Tasia's car. Tasia honked and they all waved as the car pulled away. It had been a nice visit.

Tasia was unusually quiet on the way home. Josh and Lizzie were busy bantering back and forth, providing a pleasant backdrop as she pondered her current predicament. Everything was changing again. Lizzie would be back at her dorm...Josh would be moving into his own place. She knew their roads might not be easy. Tasia sighed, recalling earlier days when, as a single gal, she had been on her own, too.

The seasons change
And with them – life
Newly emerges
Amidst the strife.

CR CHAPTER 8 ЮD

Now that she had her own apartment, the confrontations between Tasia and her mother were less frequent. But that stress was replaced with the added responsibilities of rent, car payments, gas, cigarettes, and other necessities. Food was always last on the list. On her own, Tasia just wasn't making it. If not for Ernie, she'd have gone hungry. She just needed to tough it out and hold on a little longer.

The pressure mounted and like a kettle of boiling water, something had to give. The first stab of pain in her abdomen left her breathless. She couldn't have moved if her life depended on it. Then, just as quickly, it left, only to return the next day or week. Sometimes it would linger, stubbornly refusing to release its victim. When it finally let up, Tasia would breathe – cautiously at first, then gratefully – until, like a hot sword being plunged into her flesh, the searing pain would hit again. It seemed to strike mostly in the evening hours. Ernie would helplessly hold her till it passed.

After several tests and x-rays, the doctor explained, "For whatever reason, parts of your colon occasionally perform spasmodically, almost like a knot being tied and then released." Her heart and hopes sank as he added, "Spastic colons never heal. You'll always suffer to varying degrees from it."

The condition could be helped by pills, much to Tasia's relief. Although the medication eased her symptoms, true to the doctor's word, the underlying condition would intermittently manifest itself unpredictably. Just another thing to learn to live with. Tasia tried to connect the disjointed pieces of her life, much like one sits down and tries to assemble a scattered jigsaw puzzle.

Springtime settled in, and the warm rays of sunshine streamed through the top windows of her cramped basement apartment. Outside the windows she could see the cracked, uneven sidewalk as traffic buzzed along the street above.

One Saturday afternoon as she sat in bed reading, her grandmother called. She smiled in surprise. Her grandmother had never telephoned before. When they did talk, it was either in person at a family gathering, or because Tasia had called her.

Their conversation was longer than usual that day. Nearing the end of it, Tasia's grandmother said, "I always felt that your mother needed special attention when she was a young girl. Even as an adult, I've always tried to be there for her, more so than my other children. Tasia, I've seen how angry she can get with you and I know that sometimes it's been hard for you. Deep in my heart, I know you're really not a bad girl. Always remember that I love you, Tasia."

Tasia thanked her, hung up the phone, and cried. She *was* loved. Trying to be strong and yet still keep pushing ahead was hard to do. So much to overcome, both emotionally and physically. Well, step by step, she would walk her pathway through life. She just needed to hang in there.

Thank God for Ernie. They would be married in July – almost a year to the date from when they had met.

In love He covers and adorns His bride
Until the day the trumpet sounds;
His loving arms enfold and protect
Within my sightless bounds.

☙ CHAPTER 9 ❧

Most girls dream about what their wedding will be like. Tasia couldn't remember ever dreaming of hers as a girl. No, to dare to dream could only open the door to more disappointment. But now, with Ernie, she allowed herself that luxury.

Her mother still tried to keep tabs on her. Was it out of love, or control ... or guilt? Tasia tried to shake it off, but the ties to home remained strong.

Her parents expected a Catholic wedding, which was fine with Tasia and Ernie. Unfortunately, Ernie's ex-wife was Catholic. Since Ernie's previous wedding had taken place in the Catholic Church, an annulment of that marriage was required for Tasia and Ernie to be married with the Church's blessings.

It seemed silly to her. How did one make a pronouncement that a marriage never happened, when, in fact, it did and a young son existed as evidence?

They went to see a parish priest. Not having made an appointment to see anyone in particular, Tasia smiled broadly when she recognized Father Stanley at the rectory's large double doors. Tasia knew him from attending grammar school. *Good, that might work in our favor.*

"Hi, Father Stanley, good to see you again," Tasia said, extending her hand to shake his. "Remember me, Tasia? And this is my fiancé, Ernie."

"Yes, hello, Tasia," Father Stanley said warmly, taking her hand and shaking it in his larger one. "It's been awhile." Then, turning to Ernie with smiling blue eyes, he continued, "Nice to meet you, Ernie."

He shook Ernie's hand firmly. "So, what can I do for you two?"

"We had an appointment to talk to someone today about our wedding plans," Tasia said. Did he remember her confessions, as well?

An average-sized man at about five foot, seven, Father Stanley had a friendly round face and belly to match. Dressed in a casual sports shirt and pants, one would never have guessed he was a priest. Without his characteristic black shirt and white collar, he looked just like any other man.

"Come on in, then." He led the way through the mahogany doors to a study room and invited them to sit on the high-backed chairs facing his desk. The dark paneling added to the solemnity of their visit. Tasia's mouth felt dry as she forced a swallow.

After explaining the situation to Father Stanley, he rubbed his chin and thought for a moment. Since Tasia and Ernie didn't have the financial means to "pay" for an annulment, he said there was another way to possibly get Ernie's previous marriage annulled. All Ernie had to do was answer three questions. If Ernie answered correctly, Father Stanley would begin processing the annulment papers.

Simple enough. Ernie caught a questioning glance from Tasia and returned it with a confident smile. Ernie certainly was not wealthy, but he was an ethical man and agreed to answer honestly.

Leaning forward over the massive mahogany desk, Father Stanley asked, "At the time you proposed to your wife, did you have any doubt that this was a *forever* thing on your part?"

Ernie quickly stated, "No, none at all."

Shaking his balding head, Father Stanley's lips creased in a straight line across his round face. "Wrong answer. You need to think very carefully before responding to the next question."

He opened his mouth and paused, his blue eyes bore into Ernie. "On your wedding day, when you saw your wife walking down the aisle in her wedding gown, did you have any doubts or uncertainties that she was the woman you wanted to marry for a *lifetime*?"

Ernie looked straight into the inquiring, now almost imploring eyes of the priest. "No."

"Wrong answer."

Tasia turned toward Ernie and back at Father Stanley. Just what was going on here?

For the last time, the priest reminded Ernie, "Now think very carefully before answering my third, and final question."

Tasia looked intently at the priest, then again at Ernie. Father Stanley cleared his throat and repositioned himself, leaning forward in his chair toward Ernie, those eyes becoming steely blue.

"When you were exchanging your vows, did you have *any* doubts or concerns of your love for Barbara, or that the marriage might not last?"

Ernie sat straight up in his chair, his knowing gaze leveled on the priest and for the third and final time honestly responded, "No, none at all. I loved her." His word was all he had; this was one game he refused to play.

"Wrong answer," Father Stanley said with a sigh, sliding back in his chair.

Father Stanley shook his head sadly as he got up from behind the thick mahogany desk and walked toward the heavy wooden doors. "There's nothing more I can do for you."

Tasia and Ernie also stood. She had sat there quietly listening to the exchange. It was the height of hypocrisy! Now she challenged him face-to-face. "What's this all about, anyway? Did you actually want Ernie to *lie* to you just so we could get the *Church's* blessing?" The words stung even her as they spewed from her mouth. Her body tensed as she waited for a response.

Father Stanley's downcast eyes confirmed the words his mouth refused to speak.

With that, the couple walked out of the rectory, the dull thud of its unyielding doors closing firmly behind them.

One thing had been made clear from the meeting: if Tasia married Ernie, she would be excommunicated from the Catholic Church, never able to participate in any of its liturgy or sacraments. According to the Catholic clergy's viewpoint at the time, she was now doomed to hell.

You can take your religion and flush it down the toilet! Tasia thought angrily as she and Ernie stomped down the rectory steps.

The next few months were spent preparing for their upcoming

wedding. July was coming quickly. Even though a Catholic wedding was out of the question now, Tasia and Ernie still liked the idea of getting their marriage blessed by God through a minister of some sort. They checked out a little nondenominational church in a nearby suburb where Reverend Buzicross was the minister.

What a name! Tasia scheduled an appointment to meet with him.

Reverend Buzicross had a contagious smile and agreed to perform the wedding ceremony in the church's little chapel, even though Tasia and Ernie weren't members. Its cathedral ceiling capped tall, narrow stained-glass windows, adding a reverential feeling to the small limestone structure.

Unable to count on her parents for assistance, the couple would have to handle the costs of the wedding themselves. Tasia understood her parents' disappointment and the stigma with which they imagined she had branded herself. So she swallowed in surprise when her mother asked to go with her one day to shop for a wedding dress.

Tasia had been to some of the bigger, well-known stores, but wanted to comparison shop.

"Any particular places you have in mind, Mom?"

"There's a couple of shops in my old neighborhood I'd like to try. Oh Tasia, this is going to be a good day, I can feel it."

She gave Tasia directions to a little boutique just off Cermak Avenue – a modest-looking place at best. Tasia had doubts as soon as they entered the door. A smiling saleslady whose eyes crinkled with wrinkles greeted them, asking the customary questions. They were the only people in the store.

"I would prefer something simple, not poofy; something stylish, but not expensive," Tasia said. Better to be upfront rather than waste each other's time. "And I'm on a tight budget, so the less expensive, the better."

"I think I can accommodate you," the saleslady responded, through a mouthful of glistening white teeth. "My name's Sally. Please follow me and I'll show you to the fitting room."

They followed the petite woman in her mid-fifties, stylishly dressed in a white sleeveless dress with matching high heels. Sally brushed aside the curtain to a dressing room. "You make yourselves comfortable. Our bride can start undressing – let me see – about a size seven?" She apprised Tasia with experienced eyes.

Tasia nodded and began slipping off her shoes.

"Good. I'll be back soon." Sally slid the curtain shut.

In a few minutes, she brought back samples for Tasia and her mother to see. Tasia looked at herself in the large three-sided mirror in the dressing room with a critical eye as she tried on each one. The dresses were either the right price, but looked better on the hanger than on her body, or else they looked beautiful on her, but were too expensive.

"How are you doing in there?" Sally asked from the other side of the curtain.

"Fine, but I don't think any of these dresses will work." Tasia pulled back the curtain as her mother handed the dresses back to the clerk.

"Wait, I have one more that just went on sale that's your size," Sally offered, smiling broadly. "Would you like to see it?"

Tasia nodded, but didn't want to get her hopes up too high. The saleslady soon returned with an off-white dress in a silky material with a chiffon covering and long sleeves. Her mother helped button the lace neckline. A full-length veil came as part of the package. Tasia placed it on top of her head, its lace trim cradling her face. The dress fit her curves as if custom made. She looked in the mirror and saw a beautiful bride smiling back at her, hazel eyes glistening. She felt beautiful!

"What do you think, Mom?" Tasia asked, turning away from the mirror so her mom could get a frontal view.

Tasia's mom looked at the price tag pinned to the dress at the waistline. "For $95.00, I don't think you can go wrong." Then she looked up at Tasia and added softly, "It looks very nice on you, Tasia."

Tasia agreed, and Sally had herself a sale.

During the ride back home, her mom suggested, "Leave the dress with me, Tasia. I'd like it if you got dressed at home before going to the church. If you and Ernie stop by before leaving on your honeymoon, I'll make sure the dress gets cleaned and is ready for you when you get back."

"Thanks, Mom. Sounds like a good idea. We can tell you all about the honeymoon when we pick up it up."

Return rides always seem to be shorter. They exchanged pleasant goodbyes and Tasia returned to her own apartment. She smiled– her mom was with her when she had found her dress and was being so accommodating. But so much still remained to do.

Tasia and Ernie reserved Papa L'Bagio, a little Italian restaurant, for their reception. It wasn't much in the way of ambiance – no crystal chandeliers or other upscale amenities – but the price was right and the food was good. The tables could be placed alongside each other to form three long rows of seating. The buffet would consist of some pasta salads, beef, potatoes, lasagna, vegetables, and a large fruit bowl. The owner recommended a contemporary band the couple could hire inexpensively for the occasion.

The weeks went by quickly until their wedding day finally arrived. Tasia alternated between feeling light-headed and nauseous. The weight of the world couldn't have been heavier on her. Her mother was distraught. Her father just went along with the program. Every time Tasia saw her mother, she was crying—and they weren't tears of joy.

"Mom, please, don't do this – not today."

"Tasia, I can't help it. You're my only daughter. This is the day most mother's dream about, but for me, it's a nightmare!"

The photographer was busy putting Tasia through the customary pre-wedding poses. She wished her mom could share in her happiness, but refused to allow her day to be ruined. Now was *not* the time to risk an emotional confrontation with her mother. She tried to stay focused on the photographer and her upcoming wedding; not her mother's tearful, solemn mood.

So, Tasia wore her smiling face through it all and tried to distance herself from any negativity. After all, this was *her* wedding day, and after everything it took to get to this point, *she* was going to enjoy it! As long as she kept her thoughts on Ernie, she'd be fine.

After dinner, she and Ernie had the first dance and afterward busied themselves mingling with their guests as the band played, too loudly for some of their older guests, but just right for the younger set.

They danced late into the evening, then left for their hotel room at the local Holiday Inn. Ernie carried his new bride over the threshold. The heady fragrance of roses wafted across the room as her foot touched the floor. Ernie had arranged for a vase of twelve long-stemmed red roses to be delivered to the room earlier that evening. Although he didn't have much money, he wanted to make their wedding night as special as he could for her. Tasia's heart was warmed by his thoughtfulness, as they settled into bed for their first night together as husband and wife.

Early the next morning, Tasia and Ernie headed off to Florida for their honeymoon. Blue sky and sunshine! Perfect weather for a road trip in their convertible. A song played on the radio, "Zippitee dooda, thank you, Lord, for making him for me ... I'm the happiest girl in the whole USA!" Tasia sang along, making up her own words to the verses as Ernie turned to her and smiled.

Her past was behind her now. She'd been given a new lease on life. Ernie loved her and she, him. How wonderful to be loved without expectations or fear of reprisal.

For the first time in her life, she allowed herself the luxury of feeling free – even if just for the moment. Oh, how sweet it felt!

"I know the plans that I have for you,"
Says God, her Father, above –
"To give you hope and a future bright,
Wrapped up in My love."

CZ CHAPTER 10 ßO

What a glorious honeymoon. After driving through the Smokey Mountains, Tasia and Ernie drove down to Jacksonville, Florida and flew to the Bahamas in a little propeller-driven airplane. It had been so relaxing, so wonderful just to enjoy being alive and loved.

All too soon, the daily grind beckoned them home, but this time life would be different. This time, she was not alone.

True to their word, upon returning from their honeymoon they stopped by Tasia's folks' house to relay some of the highlights of the trip and to pick up her wedding dress. Her mother smiled, her gray eyes sparkling, and invited them in. It wasn't long before the subject of the wedding dress came up.

"The veil and dress were so wrinkled," Tasia's mother said, while standing in the doorway between the dining room and the living room, "that I decided to iron them for you." Without hesitating, she continued, "Unfortunately, the iron setting was too hot for the material and burned right through it."

Tasia looked at Ernie, a knowing exchange passed between them.

"The same thing happened to the veil," her mother continued in a dry tone. "There was nothing else that could be done, so I threw them out. I'm sorry."

"The dress *and* the veil?" asked Tasia, gripping Ernie's hand.

"Yes," her mother replied, her squinted eyes and upraised brows challenging Tasia.

Tasia stood stunned, and had just opened her mouth to respond when Ernie took hold of her arm and motioned toward the door. "Good-bye," he said in a polite tone and hurried her out the door toward his car.

"I can't believe what just happened!" Tasia exclaimed as they drove off.

"Listen, now that she's had her retaliation, maybe she'll be satisfied," Ernie said, glancing in the rear view mirror. "Besides, what's done is done."

"Easy for you to say." Tasia had heard those words before. When…? Ah yes, the night of her engagement. *Dé jà vu.*

They rode in silence the rest of the way home. By the time they reached their destination, Tasia's thoughts turned to the business of unpacking. They had picked the new apartment for its close proximity to the expressway and low rent. With just a living room, bedroom, kitchen, and bathroom, it would do for the short-term. They were willing to scrimp a little now in order to get a financial foothold for their future.

The first weekend Pete spent with them as a married couple, Tasia and Ernie gave him a bath and discovered that his scalp was thick with scales of dirt. Even his toenails had grown around and under his toes!

The newly married couple also acquired a six-week-old, seal-point Siamese kitten, which they named Pandy. She was given to them as a gift by one of Ernie's co-workers. Ernie wasn't much of a cat lover, but when he heard that Pandy had been deserted by her mother, he acquiesced. She was such a skinny little thing – white with the traditional brown markings on her ears and face – and full of spunk! Pete enjoyed playing with her and ran to see her whenever he was over.

One Saturday morning, they picked Pete up from his great-grandmother's house. Pete had been sick for several weeks and hadn't been getting better. This time, however, Barbara allowed Ernie to come for him.

Pete looked uncommonly pale, was slightly feverish, and his cough sounded like it came all the way from his toes. His little belly stuck out just like the distended bellies of the children she had seen on television commercials.

Ernie rubbed his head, his thick eyebrows drawn together in concern. Drawing Tasia aside, he spoke softly near her ear. "Honey, Pete needs medical attention. Do you know any doctors in this area?"

"There's a health clinic a couple of miles north of here that I used to go to as a child," Tasia whispered to Ernie. "Do you want me to go with?"

"If you think you can handle it, I'd prefer not to go. Doctors and me don't mix," Ernie responded, frowning harder.

"All right," Tasia said. Pete sat engulfed by the couch like an orphaned waif.

After examining the young boy, the young, blond-haired doctor stood back to his full height, his piercing blue eyes examining Tasia, and snapped, "Your son has malnutrition and is very ill. He wouldn't be so sick if you fed him properly." Looking back toward the scrawny child, he added, "You should have brought him in *much* sooner."

"Doctor, you don't understand," Tasia protested. "*I'm* not his mother. And the reason I brought him in is because I *am* concerned about him."

She went on to explain that she and her husband only had weekend visitation rights, and that concern for Pete's health had brought them to the clinic. The doctor's stern face loosened somewhat.

Pete was diagnosed with bronchitis and malnutrition. That was the last straw! Ernie and Tasia discussed having Pete come live with them permanently.

When they dropped Pete off, Ernie confronted his ex-wife. Tasia stayed with Pete in the parlor, but could hear every word. "Barb, this just isn't working and Pete's the one suffering for it. You don't have the time to care for him, and though your mother and grandmother have good intentions, they're too old."

Barb volunteered, "I've been thinking about it, too. If you and Tasia want to draw up change-of-custody papers, I'll sign them. It's time for me to move on with my life anyway. I'd like to have the right to visit Pete every now and then, though."

During their ride home, Tasia said, "I don't know, Hon. It's going to be confusing enough for Pete adjusting to his new life with us without Barbara popping in and out at her every whim." She reached over and touched Ernie's leg. "I just don't think it would be in Pete's best interest. Just let the door close."

Ernie focused on the road, his dark brown eyes narrowed in thought. "I disagree, Hon. I think Barbara has a right to see Pete – after all, she *is* his mother. I'm sure she wouldn't do anything to cause him further upset." Ernie glanced over at Tasia and took hold of her hand, squeezing it gently.

"All...right," Tasia said. "After all, you *are* his father." She hoped he was right, but her instincts told her otherwise.

Sometimes I can scarcely stand –
The magnitude's so great!
Other times, more gentle lappings
Cause me to contemplate.

CR CHAPTER 11 ꙮ

Leaving Josh and Lizzie to sleep in, Tasia attended the morning service at her church. Her heart always warmed to see little ones with their parents. She ran into some friends of hers there who had just recently adopted a little five-year-old girl from China. Their little girl was an answer to their prayers, fulfilling a desire for a daughter of their own and offering that little life a second chance. Tasia wondered how much she'd remember. If her own experience with Pete so many years ago was any indication, they could be in for an uphill climb. Even now, she found herself shaking her head at the very thought of it all.

She glanced at her watch as she briskly walked to her car, beating the rush. *Twelve-twenty. Josh and Lizzie should be up and about by now.*

The church service always filled her soul. She loved singing the familiar melodies that so inspired and lifted her spirit. The message was about the importance of family, comparing our earthly fathers with our heavenly Father. Afterwards, Pastor Tom had prayed a special blessing over them all.

Tasia found her Saturn in the parking lot. *Twelve-thirty. Not too bad.*

"Hi, guys, I'm home!" Tasia called out as she opened the door.

"Hi, Mom," Josh said sleepily, lounging on the couch in his pajamas.

"Where's Lizzie?" Tasia asked, reaching down to replace her shoes with her blue terrycloth slippers.

"Still sleeping, I s'pose," he said, glancing in Tasia's direction while flipping through stations.

Tasia climbed the stairs, patted Josh on the shoulder, and continued up to the bedrooms. "Lizzie, you up yet?" Tasia asked, rapping gently on Lizzie's door.

"Am now," came the half-awake response. Tasia heard the rustle of bed covers being turned.

"Good. I'll start fixing breakfast. The sooner you get in gear, the better." Tasia turned and started to walk back downstairs to the kitchen.

"Huh? Oh, yeah – shoppin'. Okay, be up shortly." A loud, drawn-out yawn sounded as Lizzie thudded out of bed.

Apparently, waking up was hard to do. "Okay," Tasia called out with a smile.

She busied herself in the kitchen, humming as she prepared breakfast. The salty-sweet smell of sizzling bacon brought Josh into the kitchen. "How was church?"

"Fine. Pastor Tom talked about the importance of families and of good father-child relationships." Tasia flipped over a slice of puffy bacon and jumped back as it spit a hot drop of grease on her arm.

"Like I used to have…." He leaned over her shoulder, inhaling the smoky aroma. "So, what'cha making?"

"Thought some fried eggs and bacon sounded good. Don't you get too close, now," Tasia warned. "Toast or English muffin?"

"English muffin," Josh replied, backing off a bit.

"Good," she said, wiping her hands on her apron and turning to face him. "Think I'll have one, too. Can you get them started while I do this?"

"Ditto for me," called Lizzie from the stairway, still wiping the sleep from her eyes.

"You can butter your own, Lizzie," Josh retorted as Lizzie trudged down the stairs.

"Actually, Lizzie, would you pour the milk?"

"Sure, Mom." She walked passed Josh and teasingly smacked him on his shoulder. "Thanks a lot, bro."

"Anytime, sis," he said, smirking, but preparing another muffin for his sister.

Tasia put the food on their plates and they gathered around the table. The food disappeared in record time.

"Boy, I sure will miss your cookin', Mom," Lizzie said, patting her full stomach and staring at the empty plate before her.

August – the end of the summer. She just needed to get Lizzie through another year or so. No matter how tough it got, she knew Lizzie was determined to graduate. Together Tasia and Lizzie had maxed out their share of student and parent loans. Lizzie worked extra jobs during her school year to help pay her way. Tasia had planned on taking Lizzie out shopping for a few necessary items before she headed back. More importantly, though, Tasia was looking forward to spending some time alone with her daughter.

"I thought we'd go up to Spring Hill Mall," Tasia said, pushing her chair back from the table. "Josh, is there anything you need while we're out?"

"Nah, don't worry about me. I'm going to finish installing the rear speakers in the 'Stang."

Tasia picked up their plates and stacked them in the sink.

Staring dead straight at Lizzie, Josh pointed and asked, "And *who's* washing the dishes?"

Lizzie pointed right back at Josh. Tasia laughed and pointed at both of them.

The afternoon was partly cloudy, with a cool northwesterly breeze. The mall was full of shoppers taking advantage of back-to-school sales. Going to a local mall can be a good gauge of a town's residents. Tasia liked what she saw. White, Blacks, and Hispanics walked and talked kindly with each other. Rural and urban folks exchanged friendly greetings. The people seemed natural and unpretentious. She liked that about Elgin.

A new pair of shoes and a couple pairs of jeans later, they stopped to rest in the food court.

"Well, that wasn't so bad," Tasia said, sitting down at an empty table. "I know how much you look forward to shopping."

"Yeah, about as much as I look forward to finals. Guess we got lucky this time – usually I have to hit several stores before I find a pair of jeans that fit right." Lizzie set the bags down on the seat beside her. "Thanks, Mom, I appreciate it."

"You're welcome, Lizzie." Even though any savings she realized would be eaten up in finance charges, how could she not? "You thirsty?"

"No, how 'bout you?"

"Me either. It just feels good resting the ol' feet awhile." Tasia slipped off her shoes and rubbed her toes against each other, leaning forward against the table's smooth edge. "Lizzie, I'm glad we've got this time alone. There's something on my mind that I want to run by you."

"Sure, Mom, shoot." Lizzie adjusted her seat.

"Well, as you know, Kurt and I have known each other now for quite awhile and..."

"And...what?" Lizzie's full attention was on her mom.

"Lizzie, Kurt's talking about the possibility of us getting married. What do you think?" There, it was out in the open. Tasia searched her daughter's face for signs of a reaction.

"Honestly, Mom, does it really matter what I think? Kurt's a nice guy – not exactly my type – but then, I'm not the one dating him." She paused, then smiled. "Actually, the first time I met him, I had a feeling that you two would get married."

Tasia tilted her head, eyebrows raised slightly. "You're kidding, right, Lizzie? How could you know that?"

"Same way I knew about dad." Lizzie's demeanor remained steady, unmoving. "So, have you given him an answer?"

"Not yet. You're right – he is a great guy. There's no doubt in my mind that we're equally matched, but to get married again...that's a *big* step!" Tasia settled back in her chair.

"Well, if you're worried about me, don't be. I'm a big girl now, Mom." Lizzie's shoulder-length bob cradled her face, highlighting her bright hazel-green eyes.

"Yeah, I s'pose." Tasia sighed, looking back at the beautiful young woman sitting across from her. "Do me a favor, though, Lizzie, don't mention our conversation to Josh until I've had a chance to talk to him about it, too."

"Okay, Mom." Lizzie smiled widely. "I'd sure like to be a mouse in your pocket when you break the news to him!"

"You won't have long to wait. I think I'll run it by him after we get home." Tasia started to get up. "Ready, teddy?"

"Ready." Lizzie grabbed the bags.

Josh was just closing his hatchback as they pulled up into the driveway. "So, how'd you make out?"

Lizzie was out of the car first. "Great. Can you believe I actually found some jeans that fit?" She took the bags out of the back seat and went through the garage door into the house.

Tasia locked the car door. "How 'bout you, Josh – did you get it all done?"

"Yeah, finished just as you drove up." He picked up his toolbox and set it in the garage.

Tasia walked over and tapped him on the shoulder. "Hey, Josh, got a minute?"

He pivoted. "Sure – what's up?"

Tasia told him the same way she had Lizzie. "So, what d'ya think?"

Josh's face darkened and he took a step back. "What do *I* think? It's *your* life, Mom. But I've gotta tell you – every time I see Kurt standing next to you, my stomach churns. And where was he when Hershey died? *I* was the one who came through for you then. But you know, it wouldn't make any difference if it was somebody else, either." He looked Tasia squarely in her eyes, his eyes swimming in unshed tears. "God, I miss Dad so much!"

Tasia stepped over and put her arms around her son, embracing her man-child. She hadn't expected such an emotional reaction. "I know, Josh – we all do."

Josh regained his composure and straightened. "So, what'd you tell him?"

Tasia took a step back to give him some space. "I told him I needed time to think about it – to sort things out in my own mind. And that I wanted to talk to you and Lizzie about it. Most of all, though, I've got to be sure this is what God wants for me. We've come through so much, Josh – maybe it's still too much to consider."

Josh adjusted his cap. "Well, at least *that* sounds sensible. So, how come *he* hasn't talked to me about it? Or don't *I* matter to him?"

"No, Josh, that's not it. He wanted to talk to you and Lizzie first, but between everyone's schedules, it hasn't happened yet." Tasia lowered her head.

"Well, come the first of September, I'm gone. Go ahead and do what you want." He turned and walked into the house.

"Josh!" Tasia called out to him, but he didn't stop. Looking up at the ceiling, Tasia cried out, "God, I need to hear from You! If You're in this, let me know and move on Josh's heart, too."

As much as she had hoped for clarification, she was in more of an emotional quandary than before. Her thoughts drifted back to her earlier marriage.

Unconditional love, unmerited favor –
Law and grace have kissed.
Arraigned and indicted by the court –
Pardoned by Your righteousness.

CЗ CHAPTER 12 ВО

As Christmas approached, Tasia and Ernie were settling into their marriage, learning and adapting to each other's ways, interweaving their lives and dreams together in the ongoing process of becoming "one" physically, mentally and emotionally – the merging of two individuals into one complimentary unit. Though Tasia easily adapted to her role as a wife, there was a need in her life that even Ernie's love couldn't fill – a need that as of yet only now and then nibbled at Tasia's consciousness, but there nonetheless.

Peering through the veil of time, Tasia reminisced, *poor Ernie.* For only those first five months of their twenty-two years together did he have the woman he originally married.

Christmas was a time for relatives to get together, so the newlyweds paid a visit to Tasia's aunt and uncle for the holidays.

Aunt Grace, Tasia's mother's older sister, did not have any children. As Tasia was growing, she had occasionally been invited to spend a weekend with her Aunt Grace and Uncle Fred. Her aunt often remarked that Tasia was the 'daughter she never had.'

That evening, she and Aunt Grace walked toward the kitchen, leaving Ernie and Uncle Fred free to watch sports in the living room. Since neither Uncle Fred nor Ernie were exactly talkative, the television was a welcome distraction. Reassured that Ernie would not be ill-at-ease, Tasia turned and continued toward the kitchen.

She sat down on one of the green vinyl chairs tucked under the laminated kitchen table as Aunt Grace poured two cups of richly steeped tea. A few drops spilled in the process, which she immediately wiped up. Aunt Grace's house was always neat and spotless. She nonchalantly pushed her graying bangs away from her forehead, then wiped her manicured fingers on the smoothly ironed apron tied around her narrow waist.

After setting the cups and saucers on the table, she sat down across from Tasia holding a jar toward her. "Want some honey?"

"No thanks, Auntie." Tasia took a sip to test the strength of the brew. Just right. She set the cup back down on the saucer in front of her.

"I'm so glad that you and Ernie wanted to stop by and visit us tonight. So, Tasia, how are you two doing?" Aunt Grace asked with a twinkle in her honey-brown eyes. Her aunt tilted the jar, poured honey onto her spoon and stirred it into her cup, creating a rhythmic clinking sound of the spoon against its porcelain sides.

"Fine," she responded.

Something was different about Aunt Grace, but Tasia couldn't quite put her finger on it. Her normally bright eyes were actually sparkling, the corners of her lips ready to turn upwards into a smile at a moment's notice. Tasia had never seen her aunt look so joyful, and she was sure it wasn't due to her and Ernie's visit.

Her aunt leaned forward in her chair and cleared her throat. "Tasia," she began, "something wonderful has happened to me. I've recently had a life-changing experience. If I could, I would shout it out and let the whole world know! Some people shared specific truths about God to me in a way I had never understood before. I'd like to share them with you too . . . if I may." She repositioned herself in her chair and took a sip of tea.

"Whatever it is, it must be good," Tasia said with a grin, cupping her hands around the warm cup.

"Oh, it *is* good," Aunt Grace responded, sitting more erect in her chair, her brown eyes wide open and shimmering with expectancy. "In fact, it's wonderful!" She continued in a more somber tone, leaning closer toward her niece, "Tasia, God loves you so much. That's why he sent his one and only son to become a human being. He took your sins upon himself while dying for you on the cross."

Tasia scrutinized Aunt Grace carefully. She certainly hadn't expected to hear these words from her aunt – not from Aunt Grace who, like Tasia, had also been ostracized by church and family for marrying a divorced man.

Aunt Grace peered into Tasia's searching eyes as if she could read her thoughts and chuckled softly. "No, Tasia, I haven't lost my marbles…actually, I've found them." She took another sip of tea and reached for Tasia's hands. "God loves you so much, Tasia, that even if you were the only person on this earth, He still would have gone through all that so that you could be with him forever."

Tasia sat still, feeling her aunt's warm hands cupping hers, listening politely. If anyone else had been telling her this, especially after what she and Ernie had just been through with the Church, she would have walked away and dismissed it all as being just another hokey spiritual come-on. But her aunt was not a person who made decisions lightly. Aunt Grace talked about this 'God stuff' from a personalized perspective, not as a religious recruiting device. Tasia patted her aunt's hands gently, releasing their hold.

"He became the sacrifice for your sins." Aunt Grace studied Tasia. Apparently satisfied, she continued, "It's the *great exchange*, Tasia. His forgiveness in place of your sins. His righteousness in place of your unrighteousness." She reached to the other end of the table for her Bible and opened it to a bookmarked page. Then she read out loud, "For God so loved the world that He gave His only begotten Son that whosoever believes in Him should not perish but have everlasting life." She closed the Bible and set it back down on the table. "Tasia, do you understand what that means?"

Did she? All her life she had known there was a God. It would have taken a lot more faith than she had in order to believe that there wasn't. Could her concept of God have been . . . wrong? As a little girl, Tasia had been taught that Jesus had died for the sins of the world. But what her aunt was describing wasn't a "collective," impersonal salvation; this was about a personalized, one-on-one relationship.

She could comprehend, to some degree, the resolve it took to look past present pain, keeping a focus on the outcome until one's goal was attained. Her childhood, indeed her marriage to Ernie, were prime examples. If she could be anything, she could be resolute. Jesus had exhibited that resolve in the events leading to his crucifixion.

Even the nuns at grade school had drilled that story into her. Her resoluteness, however, had usually not been motivated by that kind of love.

Something clicked for Tasia and things began to make sense. She didn't understand *all* of the ramifications of such a decision. How could anyone? But she did understand that kind of resolve. The fact that it was motivated by a loving God on her behalf, instead of an angry, judgmental being impacted her in a way that nothing before ever had. Tasia had learned about God in an intellectual, collective sense as a child, but she had never thought of identifying *with* him on a personal basis before tonight.

Tasia closed her eyes and could feel his love and acceptance extending out toward her. Finally, someone had given her the piece to the puzzle that had been missing for so long. She wanted this gift from God-this Jesus-in her life permanently.

God really does love and care about me, she realized silently. *Lord, I need you in my life,* she prayed. Joy began to flow into her heart as the greatest exchange in her life occurred. Not until this moment had she ever been so touched by love!

Aunt Grace smiled.

Tasia felt like a new creation. She couldn't wait to tell Ernie about it on their way home that night. This was exactly what Ernie needed.

With final good-byes and hugs exchanged, Tasia and Ernie left. They got into their car and Ernie started the ignition. Tasia turned and waved goodbye to the shadowy forms of her aunt and uncle silhouetted against the light of their living room window.

"Honey," Tasia began, "Aunt Grace told me some things tonight that I can't wait to share with you."

"I'm all ears," he replied, pulling away from the curb and honking twice to signal goodbye.

Enthusiastically, Tasia repeated the parts of her aunt's conversation that had impacted her the most, then waited for Ernie's response. Surely, he would want in on this, too. Who wouldn't? Who would want to go through life without knowing Jesus as their personal savior and lord, and experience his love and joy, too?

Ernie shifted uneasily in his seat and combed his fingers through his hair. "Honey, I love you, but I've heard it all before. After all, remember ... my younger brother and I were raised in a nondenominational orphanage in Philadelphia. Every day at Girard we had to attend chapel after breakfast. I had the Bible crammed down my throat there. In fact, I probably know more about the Bible than you'll ever know." He reached for her hand, glancing quickly at her before returning his eyes to the road. "I know you're level-headed, Honey. You'll get over this."

She gulped and sat back. "No, Ernie, you don't understand – this isn't something you 'get over.' I hope I *never* get over this." Tasia paused. He just wasn't ready. She softened her voice. "I just thought I'd share it with you, Honey, that's all." Tasia watched Ernie's profile for a reaction, but he remained impassive.

"That may be good for you, but I don't need Jesus as a crutch in my life," Ernie replied, pulling his hand away from hers, grabbing the steering wheel to maneuver around a pot hole.

Tasia could hardly believe what she heard. *A crutch?* "Honey, this is so much more than having Jesus as a crutch. This is about *forgiveness*, eternal life – *unconditional love!*"

Ernie's face showed no emotion. He faced forward, eyes on the traffic. "Tasia, as far as I'm concerned, this conversation is over."

Tasia felt as if cold water had just been poured over her, yet she still felt peace within. Her aunt had warned her that salvation was not something that could be wished or forced on anyone. Each one had to receive it as a gift, just as she had. God's love had touched her. She would just have to trust that His love would eventually touch Ernie as well.

That moment marked the beginning of a spiritual journey Tasia would walk alone. Although physically united and building their marriage together, would they inevitably drift further apart spiritually, borne on currents traveling in different directions?

While at its pinnacle
Of glory unfurled –
The flower is plucked
From its own little world.

○ℰ Chapter 13 ℰ○

Tasia held onto the hope that relations with her parents would smooth over after the wedding. As the months passed, however, it became painfully apparent that they wouldn't.

Ernie hurried home from work one day and rushed through the door. Before even taking off his jacket, he lifted Tasia in his arms and kissed her excitedly. "A position has been offered to me out on the West Coast, with equal pay, if I – if we – want to transfer there."

As she landed back on her feet, Tasia exhaled and leaned her chin on her hand in contemplation. "Well, the custody case will be over soon. This *would* give us a chance for a fresh start with Pete..."

"Without the emotional roller-coaster of family encounters," Ernie pointed out.

The timing seemed perfect. The court hearing was three weeks away. On a Wednesday, Tasia gave her bosses two-weeks' notice. Once the custody order was signed, Ernie planned to pick up Pete after work that Friday. They would rent a Ryder truck early the next morning, load it up and start down the road toward their new beginning. Tasia, Ernie, Pete, and their Siamese cat, Pandy – one big, happy family.

That was the plan.

The judge signed the custody order, making everything official. Tasia used her time off from work to begin packing.

Ernie enjoyed his job as parts manager at Glenlake Volkswagen and hoped to make the transition as easy as possible for his replacement. When Friday morning rolled around, he said to Tasia, "Honey, I need to go into work today to finalize some things." He gulped down the last of his coffee before heading toward the door. "I won't have time to pick Pete up today."

Tasia shook her head, letting out a long sigh. "Well, if you must, you must. It'll just wait till tomorrow then."

"Hon, there won't be time for me to get him tomorrow, load the truck, and still keep to our time table. Please?"

Traveling to pick up Pete was a two-hour ride round-trip, not to mention possible delays in gathering his belongings and saying any goodbyes.

Ernie hadn't needed to ask – Tasia saw the request in his questioning eyes – those beautiful brown, trusting eyes. "I just don't feel comfortable going alone though, Ernie," she responded, putting an apple and a salami sandwich in his lunch bag.

"It'll be okay, Hon. I just don't see any other way." Ernie patted her shoulder reassuringly.

"Yeah, you're probably right," Tasia conceded, after a long pause. "I'll just go, get Pete and hurry back home." She handed Ernie his lunch.

Ernie took the bag from her hand and his face relaxed. "Thanks, Hon, after all, how bad can it be?" He gave her a quick kiss goodbye, opened the door, and went on his way.

Yeah, how bad could it be? Tasia gently closed the door after him.

She knew the route by heart, and was soon at Pete's great-grandmother's house. Checking the cars parked along the street, she noticed Barbara's wasn't among them. She breathed a sigh of relief.

As she parked the car, she sensed something wasn't right. There was no apparent explanation for it – physically, she felt fine. This was something deeper – a warning in her spirit – that she shouldn't go in. But, she had no choice. Inhaling deeply, she opened the car door and got out, resolutely plodding toward the house. A cool spring breeze played with her hair, scattering it in different directions.

Tasia carefully walked up the cracked cement stairs of the front porch and rang the chipped plastic doorbell.

Barbara, her mother Laverne, and grandmother Nana were some of the last holdouts in the racially changing neighborhood. They had decided to stay no matter what. Nana's house was badly in need of repairs. The peeling, grayish-white paint had withstood more than its share of winters. Though there had been some violent skirmishes involving other Caucasians, for the most part, their new neighbors tolerated the women's presence.

A few minutes later, Pete's great-grandmother answered the front door. Her wrinkled left hand cracked the warped wooden door open just enough for her gray head to poke out. Looking past Tasia toward the direction of her parked car, she demanded, "Where's Ernie?"

"He had some things to wrap up at work and couldn't come."

Nana winced against the sunlight, then glanced at Tasia again. Sighing, she slowly opened the door wider to let Tasia in. Pete sat by himself in a corner of the dark room.

Tasia greeted him with a warm hug. All they needed now was to get his belongings and be on their way.

"Pete, do you have all your stuff together?" Tasia asked while watching Nana's hunched-over silhouette out of the corner of her eye.

The response came from another corner of the room, and not in the voice she expected. Barbara emerged from the shadows. "It's taking more time than we expected. Have a seat, Tasia. It shouldn't be much longer."

Tasia sat down on the couch, sinking deep into its worn-out cushions, feeling about as comfortable as a lobster trapped in a kettle of boiling water.

If they wanted to drag this out, she couldn't let them. This was hard enough. Tasia struggled up from the cushion's soft grip, stood, and matter-of-factly stated, "I'm on a tight schedule and can't stay very long."

Pete's grandmother, Laverne, turned toward Nana and Barbara, saying something in a quiet undertone. Whatever she said helped move things along.

Soon, all of Pete's clothes, toys, schoolwork, and personal records were boxed up. For a five-year-old, Pete didn't have very much. All his life's belongings fit into a couple of boxes. That was a good thing since she wound up carrying them out to the car by herself.

With the last box safely stowed in the car, Tasia returned to the porch. "Well, Pete," she said, "it's time to say goodbye." Tasia looked at the three women standing there. So far, so good. "Thanks for all your help."

Laverne and Nana took turns hugging and kissing Pete goodbye, followed lastly by Barbara. She clung to Pete, telling him repeatedly how much she loved him and didn't want him to go.

Pete hugged her back. "I love you, too, Mommy. Don't worry – I'll be back again."

Several minutes passed. The awkwardness of the moment was taking its toll. Barbara obviously was not going to make this easy.

"We need to be going now," Tasia said to Barbara, edging closer to her and Pete.

Seconds passed, seeming like minutes. Barbara was frozen in place, kneeling next to Pete. Her face was buried in his bony little chest and her hands gripped his skinny forearms, as if she would never let go. Pete stared at her with wide eyes, his little brow furrowed.

What kind of game was Barbara playing now? How was she going to get Pete out of there without causing him any more confusion or pain?

"We really need to go *now*," Tasia stressed.

Still no change!

Tasia deliberately reached for Pete's hand. "Come on, Pete."

Pete looked up at Tasia. Without saying a word, he extended his hand. Then he looked back at his mother. Barbara reluctantly released her hold and they began to slowly move away from her. Tasia held Pete's hand tightly in her own.

They were about half-way between the house and the car, when a sudden shriek came up from behind them. "How dare you take my son from me!" Barbara shot down the porch stairs, ran to Pete and snatched his free wrist in a vice-like grip.

This wouldn't have happened if *Ernie* had been here, Tasia thought. She continued moving toward the car, breaking Barbara's hold. "Come on, Pete," she encouraged.

"You're taking *my baby* away from me!" Those words sliced repeatedly through the air as Tasia and Pete neared the curb.

What could Tasia do? She hadn't thought it necessary to bring along the custody order bearing Barbara's signature, and she didn't want to get into it with Barbara in front of Pete. That would only make things worse.

Tasia chose to just keep her mouth shut and get Pete away from there as quickly as possible. "Just a little further, Pete," Tasia coaxed, inching them ever closer toward the car. "Just a few feet more.... There, we made it!" Tasia quickly helped Pete into the car, scurried to the driver's side, and took off. Glancing in the rear view mirror, she saw Barbara leaning between Nana and Laverne as if for support. Barbara had played her last card to the hilt.

Poor Pete! Tasia's heart ached for him and the damage that had been done. He sat in the passenger seat, his legs pulled up tightly against his chest, his arms wrapped around them. As difficult as it had been for Tasia, Pete was the one who had borne the brunt of that horrible afternoon's emotional firestorm.

Saturday morning came so quickly. All their preparations had led up to this moment. Tasia's two younger brothers came to help load the furniture into the rental truck. By noon, the young family was on their way to the West Coast. Destination: Sacramento, California.

Pete rode in the car with Tasia and their cat, Pandy, following behind Ernie in the large, yellow rental truck. Pete was still very somber. He petted Pandy gently, who lay peacefully on Tasia's lap. The radio played softly in the background. They finally cleared the sprawling maze of suburban houses and were on open highway. The flat stretch of road cut a straight line through vast green fields of corn.

Pete turned from the window and looked at Tasia with sad brown eyes. "Mom," (Pete had started calling Tasia "Mom" shortly after she and Ernie were married), "Why can't I stay here?"

Tasia relived yesterday's awful scene in her mind. Just how much had Pete been affected by that emotional episode? Tasia switched the radio off and prayed for an answer.

"Pete, you love Pandy, right?" Tasia asked, glancing from the cat toward him.

Pete nodded.

"Well, you know we didn't always have her. Her mommy was having trouble taking care of her. So, when she was still very young, she was given to us to raise and take care of." Tasia petted Pandy gently as the cat purred.

"At first, it must have been confusing for Pandy. I'm sure she missed her mom and her home. She had to get used to a whole new life with us. But that was good because now she knows you, too, Pete. She knows she's safe with us and that we love her."

Pete's lips pursed together as he listened carefully to her words. This was an important moment for them both.

Tasia asked, almost in a whisper, "And you know what, Pete?"

"What?" he asked, also in a soft voice, his dark brown eyes fixed on her.

"We love you too, Pete, so very much!" She reached over and pulled him closer to her side.

Pete's eyes filled with tears as he stroked Pandy's soft fur again. The car fell silent, except for the rhythmic sound of Pandy's contented purring.

With confession and directional change on your part –
Forgiveness, joy and peace He'll impart;
With healing of spirit, your body and heart –
His indwelling presence gives you a new start!

⊄ CHAPTER 14 ☋

Home – it can be many things to many people. For Tasia and Ernie, their home in Sacramento was now a rented duplex built on a concrete slab. With a six-foot high, redwood fenced-in yard, and ample living space inside, this would make a fine home for raising a new family.

In this unfamiliar location, Tasia now found herself in the equally unfamiliar role of stay-at-home mom. Added to the much s-l-o-w-e-r pace of life in Sacramento generally, this was quite an adjustment for her. Before Pete started first grade in the fall, he and Tasia would often take walks or car rides around the neighborhood to familiarize themselves with their new area. Because Pete's grandmother had not allowed him to play with other children, he lacked normal five-year-old social skills and was unfamiliar with children's play activities.

Ernie's father had died unexpectedly when he was seven, leaving him to grow up without a father figure. Because of that, he desperately desired to be a good father to Pete. But their relationship also suffered from Pete's lack of inter-relating skills. When Ernie wanted to roughhouse or play catch with his young son, Pete just didn't know how to respond or what to do. The ending was always the same – one of them would walk away. So Tasia began working with Pete, practicing throwing and catching a rubber ball to improve his eye/hand coordination, and hopefully his relationship with Ernie, as well. Besides, Ernie's birthday was approaching. Birthdays should be special and Tasia hoped to make this one extra special for Ernie.

After a particularly long day at work, Ernie smiled as he walked into the living room. After singing 'Happy Birthday' and serving him his favorite dessert, Boston cream pie, Tasia announced, "We have a surprise for you!" She and Pete got up from the table and walked a few feet away from each other. Tasia gently lobbed the rubber ball to Pete and he caught it. Tasia clapped her hands in triumph and Pete's grin filled his entire face.

Ernie got up from the table, clapping also. Now it was his turn. But when Ernie tried lobbing the ball to him, Pete missed it. "That's okay, Pete – just keep your eye on the ball," Ernie said, holding up the blue rubber ball as reinforcement.

Pete nodded, tossing the ball back to his dad.

Ernie caught it and was ready to try again. "Okay, here we go. Ready, Pete?" Ernie held the ball out in front of him for Pete to see.

"Yeah, Dad." He looked to Tasia, his eyes wide as he shuffled his feet.

She knew how much he wanted to please his dad. Tasia smiled and nodded to him.

Ernie tried again. Pete missed. After two more unsuccessful attempts, they both lost interest in trying – again.

That unfortunate little display was similar to the ongoing hit-and-miss relationship that carried on between them. When Ernie would reach out to Pete, Pete wasn't able, or willing, to reach back. And similarly, when Pete tried to reach out to his dad, Ernie wasn't able, or willing, to reach Pete at his level.

Autumn soon arrived in the Sacramento valley. Some of the trees began losing their leaves, but unlike autumn in the Midwest, none displayed nature's brilliant fiery hues of yellow, orange, and red. Straw-dry, yellow fields turned a deep shade of emerald green as the region absorbed its rainy season. Grey clouds lining the horizon competed against the distant Sierra Nevada foothills surrounding the valley.

Pete looked forward to starting first grade at his new school. If he had any reservations at all, they vanished somewhere between Tasia's accompanying him on the morning walk and the afternoon dismissal bell.

Her time at home offered Tasia new opportunities. Among other pursuits, Tasia used the quiet hours at home to hone her domestic skills. By now, she had met a few neighbors, one of whom took a particular interest in Tasia and encouraged her to sew.

Living solely on Ernie's income, money was tight. Tasia managed to save thirty-five dollars to buy a thirty-year-old portable Singer sewing machine that was on sale. Soon, she was making curtains and simple outfits for Pete and herself.

Tasia also drew closer in her relationship with God. Aunt Grace had given her a Bible. During the quiet moments after everyone left in the morning, Tasia loved to sit in the warm sunshine streaming through the glass patio door and just read or talk to God. Those were special moments.

One day, Tasia read a verse about forgiveness, "For if you forgive men when they sin against you, your heavenly Father will also forgive you. But if you do not forgive men their sins, your Father will not forgive your sins."

What did this mean for her? Did she need to forgive her mother? The answer flashed across her mind in an instant. *Yes.*

"How can I, Lord? You know what went on."

As she sat in quiet contemplation, tidbits from earlier conversations with her grandmother began to form a pattern in Tasia's mind. Her mother had been a slow learner. Having been born with poor vision had also taken an emotional toll. Growing up, her mother had often been the brunt of cruel jokes. She always had to try harder than most people. Keeping everything methodical and regimented helped her to make a go of life.

Tasia began to see her mother through fresh eyes, God's loving eyes. The crusty hardness of her heart's attitude toward her mother began to soften, dissipating like a heavy fog in strong sunlight.

Another thought popped into Tasia's head: *write a letter of forgiveness.*

Is that from you, Lord?

"Lord, You're going to have to help me then." Tasia sat down and prayed. Images and emotions began to surface from her childhood. With each painful recollection, Tasia pictured herself handing it over to Jesus, his arms stretched out wide on the cross to receive it. It was a tough exercise, but with each recollection, Jesus administered grace and healing to that memory.

Tasia didn't cognitively recognize what was happening within her during this process. She just knew Jesus had exchanged her hurts, filling her with peace. It felt so good.

Something broke her reverie. Tasia looked at the pendulum clock hanging on the wall. One-thirty. Pete would be home from school in a couple more hours.

She picked up the pen and began:

Dear Mom,

The Lord has laid it on my heard to write you a letter.

"Okay, Lord, now what do I write?" Tasia asked aloud.

Last Christmas, I accepted God's forgiveness in Jesus. He's forgiven my sins and given me the peace that comes from a new life in Him. That gift is available to anyone who wants it. Mom, I'd love for you to experience that same peace, too.

"Okay, Lord, what next?" Tasia leaned forward in her chair and wrote: *Mom, I just want you to know that I forgive you for all the hurt you caused me.*

"There, Lord, it's done," Tasia said. As Tasia reread what she had written, the thought came to her that she wasn't done yet. *Ask her to forgive you.*

"Lord, You don't understand," Tasia replied. "*I* was the one who was hurt."

Gently, she was reminded that forgiveness worked both ways and Tasia felt compassion well up inside as her heart melted.

And Mom, please forgive me for all the hurt and disappointment I've caused you. I know I wasn't the daughter you expected or needed.

Love,

Tasia

There – it was done. A brief letter, but each word was long in meaning. Tasia licked the envelope shut, put a stamp on it, and walked to the mailbox at the corner of the block. Slowly, falteringly, she opened the mailbox slot and extended the envelope toward it. The envelope was halfway in. She felt dizzy and weak-kneed. "Lord, this is hard! Once I let go of it, there's no turning back!"

Still, Tasia knew she had to go through with it. She didn't want to be burdened with things anymore. She didn't want anything to stand in the way of her relationship with this God who so wanted her to be free.

Tasia released her hold on the envelope, and on her past, and ambled back to the duplex. "Whatever happens now is in Your hands."

Opposing destinations –
One leads to life, one to death.
Forces in opposition –
Diametrically dissent.

C၆ Chapter 15 ၈Ⴢ

"It's in Your hands." Tasia now spoke those same words once again, but this time in a different context.

She and Kurt were on their way to Shabbat, the Friday night service at a messianic Jewish fellowship in Lake Zurich. She and Kurt started attending Sar Shalom with their friend Robin, a Messianic Jew. Down through the centuries, Y'shua and his church had become uncharacteristically gentilized. People knew him now as Jesus, the Greek version of his name. Like so many others, Kurt had never been exposed to the Jewish roots of his faith before, and it opened up new vistas of understanding as they met for Bible study and song led by pastor-teacher, Michael Rydelnik. Michael was a man short in height but large in stature who had grown up in New York, the son of two Jewish parents. He recalled how, even as a young boy, so-called 'Christians' had wounded him both verbally and physically, accusing him of being a Christ killer. As a young man possessing a keen intellect, he had confronted the rabbis concerning key passages in scripture he had discovered that clearly described the time of Messiah's appearance and crucifixion. If the scriptures were true, Jesus *was* the Messiah. It revolutionized his life and transformed him.

Kurt held Tasia's hand as they wound through the curving roads leading to Sar Shalom. He squeezed it gently and glanced at her. "You're more quiet than usual, tonight, Tasia. What's on your mind?"

"Already you're beginning to read me like a book." Tasia laughed and caught his glance. "I was just thinking about the kids. Lizzie's only been gone a couple of days and I miss her already. Tomorrow's the first of the month and Josh'll be moving out into his apartment."

"Did you convey my offer to help?" Kurt asked.

"Yeah – he said 'thanks, but no thanks.' Some of his buddies'll help out. Anyway, it's not like he's got a lot of stuff to move, you know."

"Right. Well, with all these changes going on, Tasia, just remember, I'm here for you." He turned and smiled at her quickly before changing lanes.

His smile had such a way of warming her heart. Tasia continued, "Last weekend, I mentioned to Josh and Lizzie that you had brought up the 'm' word with me. I wanted to get their reactions – boy, did I!"

Kurt turned and looked at her briefly. "So are you going to keep me in suspense or what?"

Tasia's smile faded along with the waning sun. "Josh took it real hard. He said he would have preferred it if you had approached him first."

Kurt's smile dimmed as well. "Tasia, if I could have, I would have. His wounds are taking longer to heal. And what about Lizzie – what'd she say?"

"Lizzie didn't seem all that surprised about it. Actually said she thought you were kind of nice." As Tasia chuckled, the lilt of her voice lightened the air.

"'Kind of nice'?" Kurt's laughter blended with hers. "And what about my lady in-waiting – what does she say?" He smiled and squeezed Tasia's hand again, one bushy eyebrow raised.

"Guess she's still in-waiting," Tasia replied, returning his smile.

"As well as I'm getting to know you, Tasia, I know there's a lot more going around in that pretty little head of yours…"

Tasia cut him off mid-sentence. "Little?" She pursed her lips and pretended to be hurt, but that only encouraged him more.

"Did I mention the part about being mature and analytical?" His eyes twinkled as he glanced in her direction. "Anyway, as my love once told me, I will hold onto you this tight…" Kurt took his hands off the wheel for just a second and turned them palm-side up, open with sides joined together, "…until you get your answer." He returned his hands to the steering wheel and winked at her with a smile. Darkness was settling on the roadway, requiring more concentration and less conversation on his part.

Tasia squeezed his hand in return. She knew that she loved him. But was that enough? Enough to commit unconditionally? And what about Josh? He had once been such a happy boy....

A special name was given him –
Such a treasure in their sight;
His mother's joy, his father's pride,
His parent's combined delight!

⚬ CHAPTER 16 ⚬

Springtime had arrived in the Sacramento valley and with it a changing of the seasons, but unlike that of the Midwest, so different from what they had previously experienced. The plentiful rains colored everything a lush shade of green, unlike the torrid, hot summers where weeds were about the only things that stayed green. Tasia loved their backyard view of the foothills cresting the horizon at sunset.

The not-too-distant mountainous terrain also brought fresh opportunities for exploration and adventure. Looking for inexpensive, fun weekend outings took the young family for occasional drives to explore the foothills that cupped the valley. On one adventure, they took a walk down a sloping field of wild flowers and discovered a partially buried object not too far from the dirt road. Ernie went back to his pickup truck, got a shovel and freed it. The object was an old wooden wagon wheel with a rusty metal rim, a few spokes partially rotted away from the effects of time and weather, but still in one piece.

"Pete, can't you just imagine a pioneer family with a little boy about your age, traveling across these mountains in their covered wagon? What do you suppose were some adventures they had along the way?" Tasia picked up a shiny yellow rock that caught her attention.

Pete rubbed his pug nose and almost sneezed. "I dunno, maybe Indians were chasing them?" He rubbed his nose again and this time sneezed loud and strong.

"God bless you!" Ernie and Tasia chimed.

"Or maybe they were looking for gold," Ernie said, handing Pete his hanky.

"Or maybe they were looking for a place to stop and make a

home," Pete said. "Kinda like us?"

Tasia and Ernie looked at each other. Tasia knelt beside Pete and gave him the rock. "Yeah, Pete, kind of like us."

Pete was gaining weight and, although still a bit shorter than average for boys his age, he was making good progress at school. He even made a friend in the neighborhood and seemed happy.

Ernie's and Tasia's relationship as husband and wife was still developing, as well. Ernie still wasn't one for public displays of affection. But in the privacy of their bedroom at night, he was unreserved. Who needed July 4th for fireworks! The passage of time increased their intimacy in all areas but one. Spiritually, Tasia still walked alone.

Springtime, a time for renewal, also found Tasia pregnant, along with Pandy, their Siamese cat. In fact, everything in the Franklin home that spring proved to be fertile. Their garden grew rapidly, yielding an abundance of tomatoes and green peppers. Even the tomato worms were plump!

One evening Pete sat in bed, covered with the multi-colored patchwork quilt Tasia had made for him. Before tucking him in, she sat down next to him and held his hands in hers. "Pete, I have some exciting news for you. Sometime in November, you're going to have a new brother or sister."

Rather than the big grin she expected, Pete's eyebrows wrinkled slightly forming a frown. "Oh."

"Pete, I don't understand. I thought you'd be happy about having a new baby in the family."

"Oh, I guess so... Mom, do you love me?" Pete's brown eyes welled up with tears.

"Pete, you know I love you. You're the most important person to your dad and me." She scooted closer to Pete and hugged him close.

Pete lifted his eyes to look at her. "Then you won't love the new baby more than me?"

Ah, the moment of truth had arrived. "Pete, you'll *always* be my number one son," Tasia said slowly and meaningfully. "You'll *always* have a very special place in my heart unlike anyone else."

Pete's small shoulders relaxed and he hugged Tasia back. He

giggled as she tickled him playfully, until he finally retreated under his quilt for safety.

"Goodnight, Pete," she said, kissing him gently on his forehead. "Sweet dreams."

"Goodnight, Mom."

Tasia was fascinated with the changes taking place in her body as the baby developed to full term. She was able to buy most of the new baby's necessities from garage sales. As her delivery date grew nearer, Tasia grew nervous with anticipation.

After twelve hours in labor, Tasia saw Ernie standing in the hallway waiting expectantly as the attendant wheeled Tasia and their new baby out of the delivery room. Proudly (and exhaustedly), Tasia smiled at her husband. "Honey, it's a boy!"

They named him Joshua. Ernie liked the sound of it and Tasia liked its meaning: 'the Lord is salvation.' He looked just like a little Ernie, with wisps of dark hair and somewhat lighter features.

Aside from the occasional diaper change or feeding, Ernie didn't have very much interaction with Josh until he reached the toddler stage. That's when Josh won him over and a healthy father-son relationship began to grow.

Tasia wondered how this would affect Pete, but he seemed to enjoy his younger brother, despite the nine-year age gap. Pete sometimes offered to help with Josh, but began to fill most of his free time with a few neighborhood friends and schoolwork.

Just as life was beginning to stabilize, Ernie's full-time position was downsized to part-time. His job search ultimately led back to Chicago. Once more, a yellow Ryder rental truck and trailing automobile formed a mini-caravan. This time, they followed the long trailing ribbon of highway back to the Midwest – and to unresolved issues.

They looked for an apartment close to Ernie's new job as parts manager at Midwest Buick, and settled in a little suburb called Mt. Prospect. Ernie liked the town's respectable reputation; Tasia liked its small-town feel. They also wanted to make sure their children were in a good school district, even if they lacked the money to buy a home in the immediate future.

The two-bedroom apartment was part of a large apartment complex located right off a busy street. There was a parking lot located in the rear of the building. Some open fields sprawled nearby and schools were within walking distance, if need be. Ernie's plan was to become familiar with the area while renting and, hopefully within a few years, buy a house. The apartment would do for now.

A Bible church also happened to be within walking distance. Tasia had been content so far in her relationship with the Lord, but when she read in the Word not to give up meeting together, she knew that meant her.

"Honey, what do you think if I take Pete to a service there this Sunday? You could come along if you'd like," Tasia asked after dinner. She knew his going was a long shot, but there was always that possibility.

Ernie got up to refill his cup. "No, Hon, if you feel you should go, then go ahead and take Pete with you. I'll stay home and watch Josh." He finished pouring the coffee and rejoined her at the kitchen table. Ernie still kept his distance from God, although he was supportive of Pete attending church with Tasia.

Pastor Jackson was a fire-and-brimstone type of evangelist. A big man, standing every inch of six feet tall, he had a full waistline and a Southern accent. Tasia listened carefully to the preacher's sermons, but compared what he said to what she had learned in her reading of the Scriptures. She wanted to be sure he wasn't twisting words around for his own benefit. She didn't want to fall prey to any more deception or manipulation.

Tasia was hopeful that relations with her mom would improve now that they were back in the area. One day while visiting her folks' house in the city, Tasia and her mom moved into the kitchen to begin meal preparations, leaving the rest of the family in the living room watching television and visiting with her dad.

"Mom, did you ever get a special letter I wrote to you several months ago before we moved back?"

Her mother tilted her head and slowly shook it. "You wrote several letters, Tasia…"

"Yeah, but this one was different – in this one I apologized."

"Yes…I do recall getting that letter." Her face clouded over. "It was rather strange, though, and somewhat confusing." She turned and opened the refrigerator door. She opened the vegetable drawer and pulled out a stalk of celery.

"I wrote in that letter that I was sorry for all the things that happened between us before, Mom." Tasia paused, watching her mother separate the celery top from the stalk over the kitchen sink. Was she even listening? "Mom, I'm not the same person I used to be. I've accepted Jesus as my personal savior."

"I don't want to hear any more about that," her mother snapped, turning abruptly around to face Tasia. "You were baptized in the Catholic Church and already belonged to God."

Tasia probably should have backed down at that point, but instead continued, "Mom, let me show you what it says in the Bible."

Her mother raised her voice, "Tasia, I *never* want to hear about this again!"

Tasia stood a few feet away from her mother. Somehow she had to try to get through to her. "Mom, this isn't the way I want it to be with us."

"How else do you expect me to react, Tasia? All your life you've always been so headstrong and stubborn. You haven't changed a bit. You don't know everything…and you certainly don't know me! You mind your tongue now, girl, and listen to me…." Her mother's eyebrows were raised to high mast and her frosty gray eyes narrowed, boring right through Tasia.

Tasia wasn't sure what to do. Normally, she would have gone toe-to-toe with her mother, but she no longer had the heart for it. Her throat constricted as she fought back tears. Then it came. She doubled over as the hot stab of pain plunged deep into her spastic intestines.

Ernie heard the commotion and came bursting into the kitchen, finding Tasia in tears. "Enough of this!" he ordered. Standing beside his wife and looking directly at his mother-in-law, Ernie declared, "This will *never* happen again. There were over 2,000 miles between us before. It can be just like there are still 2,000 miles between us and you won't see us *or* your grandchildren."

The hardness on her mother's face wilted, but she said nothing.

Tasia sat down while Ernie rounded up the kids. As quickly as the pain had come, it left. Soon they were out the door. The words had been said. Ernie had asserted himself as head of his family and Tasia's protector. Though it had been a terribly awkward situation, she was so proud her husband.

From that day on, there were no more incidents between Tasia and her mother. A new era had begun.

A daughter was born to parents who
Loved her more than life –
Guiding her as she grew up
Amidst life's joys and strife.

❦ CHAPTER 17 ❧

The coming of autumn found Tasia pregnant again, pushing Josh in the stroller, walking Pete to his fourth-grade class at his new school. She had tried quitting smoking several times before, but had failed. Once again, Tasia determined to quit. After a couple more failed attempts, she didn't know what else to humanly do, so she turned it over to God and told Him that if she ever took it back, He could kill her. Whatever psychology was involved in that, Tasia wasn't aware of at the time. All she knew was that she no longer had the cravings. God was doing His part, she would do hers. From that day on, she was freed from it.

Now that they were back in the Chicago area, Pete's mother began popping in and out of his life. Did her visitations with Pete merely satisfying a lingering guilt burdening Barbara, or were there other motives? Tasia only knew what she could see. After Barbara's first visit, Tasia watched Pete withdraw into his bedroom. He only emerged when summoned for dinner.

Ernie settled Josh in the high chair and placed a bib around his neck as Tasia set the food out on the table. Pete sat and stared at his food, picking at it with his fork.

"So, Honey, how was your day at work?" Tasia sat and scooped some applesauce on a spoon for Josh.

"Well, one thing about working on Saturdays, you get more of a mix of people. For example, this one guy came in who couldn't speak English. Finally in frustration, he drew me a picture of what I guessed was supposed to be his car and pointed to something under where the hood would be." Ernie got up to get a piece of paper off the kitchen counter, pulled a pen out of his shirt pocked and started drawing. "Then he started making sounds, sort of like an engine-knocking noise. If anyone had been watching, I suppose it would have made a good comedy sketch. Finally, between hand motions, drawings and sounds, I think I finally figured out what part he needed." Ernie's smile broke into a rich, deep-throated laugh. It was contagious. Even Josh giggled in glee. Pete, however, just continued staring blankly at his plate.

Tasia looked at Ernie and then tilted her head toward Pete.

Ernie noticed. "So, Pete, what's on your mind?"

Silence.

Tasia placed a tablespoonful of mashed potatoes on Josh's tray. Josh put his hands in the gooey white stuff, lifted them to his face...and...missed his mouth. Tasia wiped the food out of his eyes and hair.

Ernie tried again. "How'd your visit with your mother go this afternoon, Pete?"

Pete looked up at Ernie, his eyes brimming with tears ready to overflow. "Oh, okay, I guess." His head turned down again as tears fell onto his pork chop.

Tasia and Ernie exchanged glances.

"What's the matter, Pete? Why so sad?" Ernie continued, "If she did anything to make you unhappy, I'll have a talk with her right now – or stop her visits altogether."

Pete looked up at him quickly. "No, Dad, don't do that. I'll be okay. It's just seeing her again after all this time, that's all. I'll be fine...you'll see."

Sure enough, as time wore on, Tasia watched Pete's emotions began to stabilize following Barbara's visits, at least by outwardly appearances.

Being back in Chicago meant Tasia was able to resume some of her old friendships, while also making new acquaintances in her neighborhood. One Saturday in November, her longtime childhood friend, Debbie, called. The two had been next-door neighbors growing up together and each one was the closest thing to a sister the other had. In fact, they were sisters – blood sisters. Back in the seventh grade, she and Debbie had each pricked their index fingers and, as their bright red blood began to slowly ooze out, rubbed their fingertips together. "Now we'll be blood sisters forever," they had covenanted. "Come on, Tas, it'll be fun. You've gotta get out a little sometimes," Debbie said. Debbie was going to get her long, curly brown hair cut and styled. "It'll be a good change of pace for you," she said, her compelling voice reaching out through the phone lines.

Tasia rubbed the back of her head. "Yeah, it would be nice to get together. We've kept in touch all these years and now that we're back, we really should try to visit more often."

They arranged to meet the next morning at a salon in downtown Chicago after Pete went to school. She would have to keep a close eye on the time in order to make it back, though, before he got home.

A while had passed since Tasia last drove in downtown Chicago traffic. Cars crawled bumper-to-bumper along Lake Shore Drive with little regard to merging traffic or blinkers signaling lane changes. The loud blaring car horns, long lines of traffic and nauseating exhaust fumes created quite a sensory experience. "Maybe next time, we'll try the train," Tasia said, winking at Josh, who giggled at the attention. "Well, at least the weather's cooperating – looks like it's going to be a beautiful day."

Fortunately, Tasia found a parking garage near the hair salon and actually arrived ahead of schedule.

Though Harry's Hair Salon catered to a more upscale clientele, she didn't find the surroundings any more impressive than the shops she occasionally visited, except for some fancy crystal chandeliers and higher prices.

One of the beautician's appointments had cancelled, so Tasia decided to splurge and treat herself to a "professional" trim, while Debbie received her services. Taking off her small gold-plated hoop earrings, Tasia placed them on her left finger behind her wedding ring for safekeeping. The earrings were just a little larger in circumference than her finger, but the ring kept them securely in place.

Josh, usually a well-behaved child, sat quietly in the stroller alongside Tasia as one of the attendants massaged the shampoo through Tasia's thick curly hair. "Oooh, that feels *so* good," Tasia said, as her nerves relaxed and her body unwound from the drive.

The experienced attendant smiled knowingly, brushing her own auburn bangs out of her eyes with the back of her soapy hand. "Even mommies need a break now and then. See? Your baby's doin' just fine," she said as a small soap bubble landed on the tip of Tasia's nose. Tasia reached up to scratch it, then slumped her head back again against the headrest.

"There, you just relax now, darlin', and let your tension run down the drain with all these bubbles."

Tasia's trim required less time than Debbie's bob-styled haircut, but soon they were back together. "How 'bout some ice cream?" Debbie asked. Bending down to play with Josh, she cooed, "He's been so good." Then, tweaking his cheeks she asked, "What d'ya think, Tas?"

Tasia glanced at her watch – almost noontime. Josh was getting hungry, but she had to make sure she got home before Pete. "Well, maybe…if we make it quick."

The ice cream shop was just down the block – a cute little place with heart-shaped, metal-backed chairs neatly placed around several small, round tables. The place was bustling with customers, and only one table was available. They quickly claimed it as theirs.

"Can I help you?" asked the waitress as they were getting seated – a young gal, perhaps in her early twenties, and from the look of her tight-fitting uniform, not in the least bit undernourished.

"Just a single scoop of vanilla ice cream in a bowl for me, please," Tasia replied. Josh became finicky and started to cry. "We're in a bit of a rush, so if you could hurry, I'd really appreciate it."

"No problem." The waitress turned to Debbie. "And you, Ma'am?"

"I'll have a root beer float," Debbie responded.

"Okay," and off she bounded, weaving through the narrow spaces between tables and customers.

"Tas," said Debbie as she pulled her earrings out of her pocket and put them on, "don't forget to put your own earrings back on."

Tasia looked down at her hand. "Oh yeah, I almost forgot about that," she said as she took her wedding ring off and set it on the table in front of her. Just as she slipped the second hoop through her left earlobe, Josh's high-pitched wail pierced the air. Tasia quickly reached down to calm him, then the two friends continued chatting, quickly catching up on old times.

The waitress soon reappeared with their order just as Josh opened his mouth to verbalize his displeasure again.

"Good timing!" Tasia reached for the bowl of ice cream. "Look what we've got, Josh," she said as she placed the bowl on the table. Tasia scooped a little bit of the cold creamy convection onto her spoon and offered it to Josh. Smacking her lips together, she hummed, "Ummmm."

Josh opened his mouth in anxious anticipation. As soon as she scooped it in, he responded in like fashion, "Ummmm."

The two friends talked away the remaining minutes, trying to fill as much conversation as possible into their short visit.

Tasia looked at her watch. "I've got to be on my way!" She strapped Josh back into the stroller, they each paid their checks and then hugged goodbye outside of the quaint little shop.

Tasia had only taken a few steps when she stopped. Her ring was missing! She ran back into the restaurant with Josh in tow complaining with every step and explained the situation to the manager. Together they walked over to the table where she and Debbie had been sitting just moments before. Tasia's heart sank down to her toes. The ring was gone!

She felt like crying and screaming all at the same time! Trying hard to compose herself, Tasia saw the waitress who had originally taken their order. "I left my wedding ring on the table. Did you see it?" she asked.

"No. Sorry, I didn't notice anything." The waitress called a busboy over. "Manuel, did you see any rings when you cleaned this table?"

"No, *señora.*"

"Are you absolutely sure?" Tasia asked him in disbelief, the lump in her throat nearly choking her.

"*Sí, señora.*"

Tasia ran her hand over the area of the table where she had been sitting. She looked around on the floor near the table, on the chair seats, under the chairs. Nothing!

Having no further recourse, and while fighting back the tears that welled up in her eyes, she left her name and number with the manager just in case someone should happen to turn it in.

They made an odd-looking spectacle. Passersby on the street stared at Tasia suspiciously, as one very pregnant, unhappy woman pushed an equally unhappy toddler in a stroller, both of them crying.

Tasia made it home just in time for Pete's arrival from school. At least that much had worked out.

How would she break the news to Ernie? Would he be understanding? Would he be angry? How could she have been so stupid? Well, there was only one way she knew to deal with it.

After Ernie came home from work and sat down on the couch, Tasia approached him. "So, Honey, how was your day?" she asked, leaning over to give him a characteristic 'welcome home' kiss.

Ernie kissed her back with one that said 'happy to be home.' "Fine." He looked up at Tasia and then frowned slightly, cocking his head to one side. "And how'd your trip downtown go? How's Debbie doin'?"

Tasia looked down at the carpeting. How was she going to break the news? "Oh, she's fine. See, I got my hair trimmed, too," Tasia managed to smile weakly as she turned around for him to see.

"Uh-huh, looks nice. How was Josh?" he asked, studying her face more carefully.

"Good as gold." Drawing closer to Ernie, Tasia sat down on his lap. The time had come. "Honey, something terrible happened today."

Ernie looked up at her.

That did it; tears welled up in her eyes.

"What is it? Did you get in an accident? Are you all right?"

"No – no accident. But, no…I'm not all right. Honey, I lost my wedding ring!" Tasia broke down and starting sobbing on his shoulder. "See?"

Ernie looked at her ringless left hand as she held it out. "How did it happen? Are you sure you're okay?"

Tasia retraced each painful detail to him. She'd already gone over it dozens of times in her mind during the trip back home. "I feel just sick about it. I'm so sorry, Honey."

Ernie patted her hand gently. "It's okay, Hon, there's nothing more you can do about it now. Anyway, the ring doesn't make you any more or less married to me. Either you are or you're not."

He was right, but being pregnant made her feel even more naked without it. If a ring is symbolic of an eternal relationship, then without it, one's heart had better stay its course all the more carefully.

Ernie's hopes were for a girl. He got his wish. Elizabeth was born just a few hours past Valentine's Day. She was just a little peanut compared to her older brother, Josh. Everybody in the family was thrilled – everybody, but Tasia. Where Josh had been a huggy, cuddly baby, 'Lizzie', as they called her, was happiest without physical contact.

One day while holding Lizzie in her arms, Tasia glanced up and saw their reflections in her dresser mirror. How sad for her, Tasia thought as her mind began to replay images of her past relationship with her own mother. She had experienced the joy of being close with her young son, Josh. Too bad she wouldn't have that same connection with this little one.

Still gazing at their reflections, Tasia suddenly realized she was falling into a trap – the old familiar trap from the mother/daughter relationship she had equated with her own life. Was that why Lizzie wasn't responding to hugs? Was she sensing, even at her tender age, that something was innately wrong with her new mother's love for her?

"No," Tasia said, the sound of determination mustering itself in her voice and even surprising Tasia herself. "History does *not* have to repeat itself!" Resolutely, Tasia spoke to the image she held, "Lizzie, I love you. I am so blessed to have you as my daughter and I'm so glad God picked me to be your mommy."

The words felt empty coming out of Tasia's mouth, sounding foreign even to her own ears. She tried repeating the phrase again, this time looking directly at Lizzie as she caressed her in her arms. Then again. With each repetition, new inroads were being made in her consciousness and in her spirit.

This became a lasting ritual for Tasia. After putting each of the children to bed at night, she would give them a hug and kiss them on their foreheads. "I'm so glad God let me be your mommy and you, my daughter" (or son, as the case may be). With the passage of time, Lizzie's returned hugs became more and more natural, although even into her adulthood Lizzie never was much of a huggy, feely type.

The relationship between Tasia and Lizzie grew into something very special and beautiful. God had truly given Tasia a fresh start. The close bond she had desired as a child, she now was able to experience with her daughter. Truly, Tasia and Ernie were blessed to have their children and to be their parents.

A robin flew into my house one day
Afraid and oh, so lost –
Earnestly searching to find the Way,
Prepared to count the cost.

CB CHAPTER 18 BD

Still confused about the situation with Kurt, she called her longtime friend. "Hi, Deb, this is Tasia…. Yeah, it has been too long. Say, I was wondering, are you going to be home at all this weekend? …This afternoon, around 2? Great – see you in a couple of hours!"

After Debbie married, she and Dan bought a home on the south side of Chicago, about a ninety-minute drive from Elgin. The mother of three active boys, she didn't have much free time on her hands these days. Tasia was happy for the opportunity to get together with her. She'd have just enough time to eat some lunch and do the drive.

At just about the stroke of 2 o'clock, Tasia pulled up to the blond-brick, two-story bungalow. Two boys were playing catch on the front lawn.

"Hi, guys – remember me, Tasia?" Looking at the oldest, "Let's see, you must be Joe. Look how tall you've gotten." Turning to the younger boy, "And you must be Jim. You were doing a good job catching that ball."

"Hi, Tas!"

Tasia looked up at the front door and saw Debbie coming down the steps. She went to meet her. "Deb – at last!" They hugged. "Can't believe how big your sons have gotten since the last time I saw them. My goodness, Deb – I can see glimpses of you in their faces."

Debbie laughed. "Don't let that fool you, Tas, they're all boy." Turning her attention to her sons, she said, "Boys, you remember my friend, Tasia? She's the one I told you has been my friend since we were young girls. Go back to playing while we go inside and visit awhile, okay?"

"Okay, Mom," they said in unison.

Tasia followed her friend inside. The place looked immaculate. "I don't know how you do it, Deb. Three boys and it still looks like House Beautiful. Where's your little guy?"

"Jeff? Oh, when Dan heard you were stopping by, he took Jeff along with him to the hardware store so we could have some time to visit." She showed Tasia to the breakfast nook. "Here, Tas, have a seat. I made some berry tea. Would you like some?"

"Sounds good." Tasia looked out the window at the backyard tree, watching the sunlight playing on its leaves. "Man, what a beautiful day."

"Yeah...getting a bit brisk, but I'll take it." Debbie finished pouring the tea and came over to the table, joining her friend. "Remember when your kids were young and we'd go for trips in the forest preserve collecting leaves?"

"Yeah, I sure do. In fact, I've been doing a lot of reminiscing lately. Remember years ago when I was pregnant with Lizzie and we met downtown to get our hair cut?"

"Wasn't that the day you lost your wedding ring, Tas?" Debbie glanced down at her friend's ringless left hand.

"Yeah, and now it's off again...." Tasia took a sip.

Debbie broke the silence. "So, Tas, how's your family doing these days?"

"Real good, Deb. Except that I still haven't heard from Pete, and don't know if I ever will. Lizzie's back at college for her senior year. She's thinking of going into social work. And Josh just moved out on his own. He got an apartment in Palatine and is splitting the cost with a friend." Tasia noticed one of Debbie's eyebrows raise and laughed, "No, Deb, not that kind of a friend."

"So, speaking of friends, how's that guy you've been seeing...Kurt? Still 'friends'? Debbie's emphasis did not go unnoticed.

Tasia smiled. "If you mean whether we're still keeping our relationship sexually pure, yes. Don't get me wrong, there's plenty of sizzle between us. But whether this relationship goes further or not, that's one thing we're both committed to." Tasia took a sip of the hot brew.

"Well, Tas – I've gotta hand it to you. These days it's not that easy – seems like anything goes. I can't imagine what it'll be like when my boys are older." She looked toward the direction of the front door.

"Yeah, I know what you mean. No, if this relationship goes forward, Deb, it goes forward in the Lord – and there's nothing either of us want to do to mess that up." Tasia turned her head, too, as the front door slammed.

Debbie's sons came inside. "Boys, everything all right?" she asked.

"Yeah, Mom, it was getting kinda chilly out, so thought we'd come in. S'okay if we go downstairs and play videogames awhile?" They carried into the kitchen the pungent, sweet smell of grass on their clothing, mixed along with sweat.

Debbie looked at her eldest. "Okay, but only for about a half-hour. After that, I want you guys to do something else."

"Aw, Mom….okay. C'mon Jim, let's go." Soon the muffled sound of their Gameboys could be heard from beneath the stairway.

Debbie turned back toward Tasia. "So, where were we?"

Tasia put both hands around her cup, warming them slightly. "Deb, Kurt's been talking about the possibility of us getting married."

"No kidding? Did he propose to you?"

"No, he's been thinking about it and wants my feedback."

"So, Tas, tell me – what *do* you think about it?" That's what Tasia liked about Debbie. She knew her well enough to ask the right questions.

Tasia leaned forward. "Deb, when I'm with him, it all seems so natural – we're so at ease with each other. He's quite the conversationalist and, more importantly, he makes me laugh. I really do enjoy being with him. Lately, he's been telling me that he loves me, and I think I love him, too – but to actually get married again? …I'm not so sure that's something I want to do again. I really like who I am now as a single woman – and as a single woman in the Lord. He's the only one I'm accountable to now and…."

"…and it's easier that way?" Debbie broke in. "But, Tas, maybe He knows you need the physical companionship, too."

"But, Deb, to love Kurt *unconditionally*? I'm not there yet."

"Isn't that what the engagement process is really all about? It's a time when the two of you grow closer toward your commitment to each other, as your relationship also grows in the Lord."

"That all *sounds* good, Deb, but sometimes it's not that easy."

"I know, Tas, I know. We've both been there." She leaned forward. "Tell, me Tas, what does your *heart* tell you?"

Tasia leaned back in her chair and sighed, rubbing the edge of the table with her fingertips as she spoke. "When I'm with him, Deb, I feel like that's where I belong. And we have such fun doing simple little things like bike riding or even just having coffee together. But then the rest of the time I have my own life that I enjoy. Maybe I like the independence of not answering to another person. And then I still have my kids to think of. And my students. If they need extra time, I can give it to them. Or if I want to do something, I just do it – like today, for instance."

"And you think you'd lose that if you married Kurt?" Debbie smiled at her friend. "Tas, if God's brought Kurt into your life, I think it would be to fill your life, not restrict it."

Tasia nodded. That made sense to her. "So, guess the thing I need to find out then is if God's the one who brought Kurt into my life or not. And if so, then it must be for a purpose, right?"

"Guess so, Tas – guess so."

She saw eagles soaring –
By life's woes unconstrained.
Then one day she joined them
And never was the same.

୯ଓ Chapter 19 ଓ୯

They made "such a nice family." At least that was what Tasia often heard. Ernie loved spending time with his family. She loved that about him. Maybe because he grew up without a father, he knew what he had missed as a child. Josh and Lizzie loved it when he would lift them up on his shoulders and plop them into their beds at night. Too big for 'horsey-back rides', Pete hadn't yet outgrown being tickled and jostled by his dad. Giggles gradually gave way to silence, as eyes heavy with sleep finally closed with the day's end. The family seemed to have jelled together into a happy whole.

Although only eighteen months separated them, Josh was two grades ahead of Lizzie. With the youngest now in school, Tasia cleaned apartments for extra money.

Tasia also enjoyed getting to know her neighbors. She found them so diverse. When she met Maggie, she knew she had found a good friend. Like so many others, Maggie had been hurt and desperately needed the Lord's touch of love. One day Maggie took part in the great exchange and invited Jesus into her life. Tearfully exposing each new hurtful memory, like peeling layers off an onion, He bathed each one of them in His healing balm. Her wounded memories were replaced with His peace. It delighted Tasia to see her friend set free.

In addition, Tasia also worked part-time at a local discount store in the evening after Ernie returned home from work. The schedule was exhausting, but worked out well for the family. Someone was always at home with the kids.

One afternoon in early October while the children were still at school, Ernie came home uncharacteristically early.

Tasia pulled the last load of laundry out of the coin-operated community dryer and carried the basket of clothes up the back stairway into their apartment. As she walked toward the bedroom, she stopped short in her tracks. "Oh, hi, Honey…you startled me. I wasn't expecting you so soon."

"Well, you'll be seeing a lot more of me for awhile. I got let go." Ernie picked up the remote control and turned on the television.

"Let go?" Tasia put down the laundry basket and sat down next to Ernie on the black vinyl couch. "What happened?"

Ernie clicked the TV off and turned toward Tasia. "Well, the dealership got sold and the new owner brought in his own people. They offered to keep me on as a parts man if I wanted. A parts man! Tasia, there's no way we could live on that kind of salary. He might just as well have fired me."

Tasia bit her lower lip. Now what?

He took hold of Tasia's hands and held them between his. "Don't worry, Honey. I'll update my resume tonight and start contacting people tomorrow. Hopefully within a few weeks this will all be behind us."

"Okay, Hon. I'll do everything I can to help us get through this, too." She squeezed his hands, got up and turned her attention back to finishing the laundry. For starters, she could save a little money by not using the dryer. As Tasia dumped the clothes on their bed to start folding, a brief, familiar stab penetrated her abdomen. "Oh no, not again!" The words were no sooner out of her mouth than another invisible dagger plunged into her intestines again, forcing her to lean against the bed for support. When it finally lifted, she remembered a verse she had read a few days earlier that made an impression on her. Reaching carefully for the Bible beneath her side of the bed, she turned to the passage and read, "Do not be anxious about anything, but in everything by prayer and petition, with thanksgiving, present your request to God. And the peace of God, which transcends all understanding, will guard your hearts and your minds in Christ Jesus."

That's what she needed – that peace from Jesus which transcends human understanding. When the next jab hit, she released her anxiety to the Lord. Immediately, His peace washed over her. She bathed in its calmness and breathed a long sigh. Over the course of the next several months and years, Tasia successfully practiced this strategic shift of consciousness until she no longer experienced the hot poker-like stabs. A condition previously diagnosed as incurable was healed by faithfully applying the word of her Creator.

Since they were already living on a tight budget, there weren't many expenses left to cut down except, perhaps, food. Instead of buying whole milk, Tasia would blend powdered milk with enough two-percent milk to make it palatable for the children. Peanut butter and jelly sandwiches became mainstay items for lunch.

The weeks went by with no promising job prospects in sight. The economy was on a downswing and jobs were hard to come by. Ernie faithfully filled out applications and left copies of his resume everywhere possible. As weeks turned into months and Ernie remained jobless, he withdrew into the escapist world of television.

"Mom, how come Dad doesn't play with us anymore?" Josh asked one day after trying to get Ernie to join him for a game of catch.

Tasia had no reply. She felt so helpless. The holidays were advancing and she didn't know what they would do.

On the day before Thanksgiving, their doorbell rang. Tasia opened the door, but all that stood on their doorstep was a shopping bag with a turkey and stuffing mix inside. A note attached to the bag identified it as a gift to them from her church.

"Thank you, God!" She quickly shared the news with Ernie.

The kids were in their bedroom playing. Pete was the first to come out after hearing the doorbell, followed by Josh and Lizzie. They ran to see what the bag contained. "Wow, a turkey!" Pete struggled to lift the frozen eighteen-pounder out of the bag.

"We're not keeping it," Ernie snapped and turned toward Tasia. "Take it back to your church and tell them we don't need their charity!" He abruptly turned his back to her, re-entering his silent world on the couch.

Suspecting that Ernie's remarks were prompted more from hurt pride than anything else, Tasia called out after him, "Then *what* will we eat instead?"

Silence.

She felt like dragging him into the kitchen, flinging open the cabinets, and giving him a good dose of reality, but thought better of it in front of the children. She knew Ernie. When he dug in his heels, not even a team of wild horses could move his iron will, least of all her.

Instead, standing in front of the television, she shattered his solitude. "Then what *will* we eat instead?"

Ernie sighed, got up and sauntered into the kitchen with Tasia in tow. After searching the nearly empty cabinets and refrigerator, he gruffly relented.

"Thank you. I know this is hard on you, Ernie. It's hard on all of us."

With their Thanksgiving blessing behind them, Tasia felt encouraged in her spirit. Surely, things would work out.

The Gardener weeds,
Cultivates and prunes –
To strengthen the plant
And produce choicest blooms.

⊂϶ Chapter 20 ϛ϶

Christmas followed on Thanksgiving's heels with still no job prospects for Ernie. Hoping to get a price break, they waited until Christmas Eve to buy their tree. The only trees left were dried-out, picked-over rejects, yet the kids helped select the best one they could find. One side of the tree was pretty sparse and bare looking. The other side was shapely and green. It wasn't a bad looking tree, and with an asking price of only one dollar, how could they refuse?

The kids were thrilled and couldn't wait to begin decorating once they got the tree home. Ernie put it up in the corner of the living room with the sparse side facing the wall. Pete and Josh strung the lights. Tasia carefully sewed popcorn and cranberries into a long strand to drape over its branches. Lastly, the final touches of tinsel and ornaments were added. Soon their Charlie Brownish tree was transformed into a beautiful, sparkling Christmas tree. The kids were so delighted with the transformation they had helped create!

After putting the young ones off to bed, Tasia placed their meager gifts under the tree: a book for Pete, a yo-yo for Josh, and a slinky for Liz. There just wasn't much money to spare for buying presents this year. "We'll just keep the emphasis on the *spirit* of the holiday this year," Tasia told Ernie, trying to keep a positive attitude, sensing his disappointment and his inability to get in the mood.

Tasia was so concerned about Ernie. He had placed job applications at every auto dealership and body shop around over these past several months, but no realistic offers had materialized. How much longer could they go on like this? "Any kind of a job at this point would be welcome, even if it's only McDonalds, just until something else comes along," Tasia said to him.

They had had several discussions about it before, but Ernie wouldn't hear of it. "Do you really think I would stoop that low? It'll be a cold day in hell before I do that!"

A person's pride can be a formidable thing, and Ernie had it in spades.

Pete and Josh woke up early the next morning and ran into the living room to see what Santa had left them. As was their custom, no presents could be opened until Mom and Dad were up and everyone was together.

Aside from intimate moments, their parent's bedroom door was usually kept open. Pete was the first to come bounding into the room, stopping abruptly where Ernie still lay sleeping in bed. "Come on, Dad!" Pete urged insistently with Josh at his side. "Wake up!"

Lizzie came running into the bedroom, a close second behind them. "Wake up, Mom!"

"All right, already!" Ernie said, pretending to be annoyed, tousling their hair. "Just let me get some coffee first."

Pete said something about snow and boxes. "Come and look!"

Grabbing Tasia's hand, Pete opened the apartment door to their front hallway. There, to Tasia's amazement, a large cardboard box stood waiting for their attention. Together, she and Pete pushed it into the living room. She carefully untaped the note from the top of the box. "Merry Christmas!" It was signed, "From the Love of Jesus" in colorful letters cut out from various magazines.

Tasia showed Ernie the note.

Ernie read the message, looked up toward the ceiling and sighed. "Go on—open it."

Inside were smaller boxes addressed to each one of the children, all in the same fashion: "To Pete, From the Love of Jesus"; "To Josh, From the Love of Jesus"; "To Lizzie, From the Love of Jesus."

Pete, never one to miss a gift opportunity, was the first to open his – a chemistry set, a new shirt and a pair of pants.

Josh, with brown eyes widening, tore into his – a train set and new outfit.

Lizzie watched her brothers open their gifts. Her happy laughter blended with their 'oohs' and 'ahhhs', but she waited until they finished before opening hers. Her patience paid off – a wooden dollhouse and a beautiful cream-colored dress with a white satin ribbon sash.

All of the clothes were the right sizes. *Who could have done this?* Tasia called a few of her friends from church – Sue, Carol, Marcia – but no one seemed to know anything about it, at least not that they would admit.

"A miracle Christmas" was how Tasia described it as time passed. To their little family, on that particular day, they had all been so touched by love. Tasia drew strength and hope from that special Christmas and tried to convey that attitude to her family. Somehow, she believed, they would get through this.

Time, however, kept slipping away. The bills came in like clockwork, demanding to be paid. Still no job prospects were in sight for Ernie.

Tasia came home one afternoon from cleaning apartments and found Ernie still in his bathrobe, sitting on the couch watching television. She was afraid he was starting to give up hope. "Honey, don't you think you'd feel better if you got dressed and went outside for a walk in the fresh air?"

"What for?"

"Ernie, you can't give up. There's too much at stake!"

Some of her friends from church stopped by to talk to Ernie. Ernie respected Scott and Sue's beliefs and considered them to be good friends. But not even they could swing Ernie around.

With each passing day, Ernie slipped deeper into a depression, becoming less and less communicative.

Inwardly, Tasia also struggled. The situation took its toll on her, too. She needed to be strong for him now more than ever, but how much longer could this go on? What about their children's needs? *Her* needs? By now, she had given up even trying to talk to him.

It became easier and easier to pretend she was asleep when Ernie's body brushed up against hers in bed, asking for a little intimate attention. How could she open her *soul* to this man who barely *talked* to her when they were standing upright? Eventually, she didn't need to pretend anymore. Ernie kept to his own side of their double bed.

As if there weren't enough challenges, Pandy got sick. Tasia knew what a special part of the family Pandy was to all of them, especially Pete. How could she not spare the money to take her to the vet? But as soon as Pandy heard the 'v' word, she refused to let anyone near her. Finally, Tasia and Pete were able to flush her out from under the bed. Josh and Lizzie got in the back seat. Pete sat up front and held Pandy firmly in his arms to prevent her from wrestling free of his grip. Pandy howled loudly for several blocks during the car ride and then became unusually silent.

"Pete, is Pandy okay?" Tasia asked.

Pete still held Pandy in a firm grip. "Yeah, Mom, she just finally relaxed. Maybe she's sleeping."

Tasia glanced at Pandy, pulled the car over and stopped. She looked more closely. "Pete, I don't think Pandy's asleep."

He looked at Tasia, his eyes open wide. "What do you mean?"

Tasia spoke to him gently. "Try to wake her up, Pete."

Pete stroked her face softly with his finger. No response. He nudged her a little harder. Nothing. "Mom, what's wrong with her?" His eyes began to moisten.

She put her hand on his shoulder. "Pete, Pandy's dead. We tried to help her, but I guess it was just too late." Tasia continued toward the vetinary hospital, but now to deliver their pet's corpse.

Pete stayed in his bedroom the rest of the day. At dinnertime, he came out and joined the rest of the family.

"Pete, how're you doing?" Ernie asked. "I haven't seen you all afternoon."

Tears formed in Pete's bloodshot eyes. "How come Pandy had to die – in *my* arms?

"Well, Pete, at least she was with the people who loved her. She was a good pet, but something was wrong inside her body. We tried to help her, but…."

"Yeah, I know." Pete didn't eat much of his food that night.

Between her various part-time jobs and keeping the household running almost single-handedly, Tasia had reached the burnout stage. Though her efforts were enough to keep food on the table and most of the essential bills paid, they fell behind in their rent. Their landlord had been very patient, but by spring his patience was at an end. When they received an eviction notice at the end of May, Tasia wasn't the least bit surprised.

How could Ernie have allowed this to happen? Keeping an appearance of normalcy for the sake of the kids was hard. But the children were much more in tune with their parents than they realized. Although the children didn't know all of the details, they were aware that things hadn't been right in their household for quite some time.

"Ernie, did you see this?" Tasia thrust the eviction notice in Ernie's face. He didn't even blink an eye, but continued watching *As the World Turns.*

"Don't you *care* what is happening? Don't you realize that come next Tuesday, we'll have *no place to live?*"

Ernie just sat on the couch, almost as if in a trance.

"Fine!" Frustration drove out any last ounce of compassion as she turned and walked away.

Tasia's heart felt cold and empty. Her love for her husband had turned into utter contempt. She couldn't even stand to be in the same room with him anymore.

Its petals are crushed,
Fragrant oil outflows –
Producing sweeter perfume
That outlasts the rose!

CHAPTER 21

That next Saturday morning, Tasia vacuumed the front stairway in their apartment building (another one of her part-time jobs). Over the high-pitched noise of the vacuum, she cried out, "God, there's nothing left! I'm emotionally and physically spent. I just can't do this anymore!" Tears of defeat rolled off her chin onto the speckled carpet beneath her weary feet.

"Your word says that there is nothing that comes into our lives other than such as is common to man, that you are faithful not to let your people experience more than they can bear, and that you will make a way of escape so that they may be able to bear it."

She paused, reflecting for an instant, and then barreled ahead. "But it's not true. God, You're not true to Your word! When they put all our belongings out on the street next week, I'm taking the kids and leaving Ernie to go live with a friend."

There, she'd said it. God hadn't struck her down with a bolt of lightning.

Tasia wiped her eyes, moving the vacuum rhythmically back and forth, grateful for the continuous roar of the motor over her words. Not that privacy would matter much come next week.

Through tears and frustration, she managed to finish her job. She walked back into their apartment, right past Ernie who sat glued to the couch. In the kitchen, she clanged some pots around noisily to get at the largest one on the bottom. Pulling open a bag of navy beans, she began preparing dinner. If Ernie even noticed her arrival, he didn't acknowledge it.

Any thought of Ernie or their situation just sharpened her resolve to be rid of him. How could she ever have loved him? They still slept in the same double bed, but miles stretched between them at night. Either Ernie was oblivious or just didn't care. Either way, she'd certainly not be the one sleeping on the couch. How long had it been since he'd talked to her—let alone touched her? *Ugh!* The very thought of him even touching her made Tasia's flesh crawl. As much as one person could love another, the coin had now flipped, exposing the hateful side.

Pete awoke early the next morning of the Memorial Day weekend and heard Tasia rummaging around in the kitchen. "Mom," he asked, approaching her with a sense of expectancy, "what time are we leaving for church?"

"We don't do the 'church thing' anymore, Pete," Tasia responded flatly, scooping coffee into the percolator.

Pete stood beside her and leaned against the white Formica countertop. "I really would like to go to church this morning."

Taking a step back, she repeated more firmly, "Pete, I told you, you don't have to concern yourself about going anymore. I know you've resisted going lately. Now you don't have to worry. We're *not going* anymore."

Tasia turned her back to him and plugged in the coffee maker.

"No, Mom," he persisted, wedging in between her and the counter. "I *really* want to go. Won't you take me?" This behavior was so unlike Pete.

He asked so earnestly that Tasia had a hard time turning him down again. "All right, Pete, but this is the last time. Go get ready. If we hurry, we can make the nine o'clock service." Under her breath she added, "And then I'll be done with it."

There was no need to wake Josh or Lizzie; not taking them along would be quicker.

When they arrived, to Tasia's surprise the pews were sparsely filled. Of course – it was the holiday weekend. She and Pete found a place to sit toward the back of the church. They had missed the song worship time that started the service. Just as well. She really wasn't in the mood. She glanced at her watch, 9:20, and hoped it would be a short service.

Soon, the slim Pastor Leonard walked up to the podium to speak. "Well, I had a sermon already planned, but this morning the Holy Spirit gave me a different message for this service. I don't know who it's meant for, but this much I do know," he paused and pointed his narrow finger, spanning from left to right as he continued, "it's meant for one of you here this morning."

"My job isn't to question why. My job is just to be obedient and deliver God's word. Hear then, the word of the Lord to you."

With that, Pastor Leonard began describing a family who was going through hard economic times, which in turn affected them in all kinds of ways.

Pete nudged Tasia and whispered, "Sounds kinda like us, huh, Mom?"

Tasia shrugged and glanced again at her watch.

Pastor Leonard reminded the congregation of the Jewish exodus out of Egypt, describing the many difficulties they faced. How they cried out to God to deliver them and how God was faithful to them in all their times of need, never leaving or forsaking them, despite their wavering faith.

Then, he got real personal. "You say God has *not been true to his word*. You say it's too late, that there's nothing left."

Tasia's ears perked up. It was as though someone put a hidden microphone in that stairway yesterday.

"Now hear the word of the Lord to you. Think back and remember how God has brought you through to this particular place in time. He did not bring you to this point just to leave you or forsake you. Stand then, just a little longer, and you will see the salvation of the Lord, even in this situation."

Perhaps another person would take that message to heart. Although Tasia knew that message was meant for her, her heart had become hard as stone. She shook her head. *I told you, God, it's already too late.*

Pastor Leonard finished by pronouncing a blessing on those present. As soon as he was done, Tasia tapped Pete on the shoulder. "Let's go, Pete." They were among the first ones out of the building.

Tasia didn't want to talk to anyone, least of all 'church' people.

"Mom, are you okay?"

"Yeah," Tasia said, smiling weakly. They rode back to the apartment in silence.

As she opened the apartment door and walked inside, Tasia noticed that Ernie was up. Josh and Lizzie were already dressed and crunching on Cheerios. Although a beautiful spring day had unfolded outside, dark clouds hung over Tasia. She couldn't stay there, she felt claustrophobic – like she was suffocating. She had to get out...fast!

"Come on guys, let's go for a walk," she said to the kids in Ernie's hearing. Something was tugging at her heart that would not be dismissed. The words of that morning's message kept replaying in her mind. Although she couldn't comprehend it, God was trying to get through to her. He was still at work in her life.

They walked about a block's distance until they reached the open field behind the apartment complex. The kids ran freely, leaving Tasia some welcome moments of solitude. She sat on the soft green grass, and contemplated the events of that morning. She felt desperate. Could she hope? *Dare* she hope again?

A tiny crack broke in the armor surrounding her heart. God still cared about her. He knew her heart. Looking up at the expansive blue sky overhead, Tasia uttered the only words she could honestly muster, "Okay, God, I'll give You one last chance."

How remarkably big of her! Ironic how self-centered the human condition is.

Although the next day was a holiday, it just another typical Monday as far as Tasia was concerned. The gnawing reality was they were only one day from eviction. Tasia made everyone oatmeal cereal for breakfast, the most nourishing meal she could afford. As usual, not a word passed between her and Ernie. Afterward, as she washed the dishes, the shrill sound of the telephone broke the silence in the room, causing her to jump.

Tasia answered the phone, handed it to Ernie and, without another thought, walked back to the sink.

The conversation lasted only a few minutes.

"What day is this?" he asked, his thick eyebrows raised.

Tasia paused in mid-wash. Was he talking to her? Hesitantly, she turned and looked at Ernie. Was he for real? His quizzical expression appeared genuine.

"Monday," she replied flatly. Didn't he even know what was going on? Did it really matter?

"That was the owner from Jacobs Twin Buick," Ernie said. "Seven months ago, I applied for a job at their body shop, but they weren't hiring. He said he came across my resume and took a chance on catching me at home today. Although he can't offer me a full-time job just yet, if I'm willing to work part-time and learn their procedures, he would offer me the manager's position. I start Wednesday."

Just like that? Tasia gasped. In an instant, their lives had turned around – and he said it all so matter-of-factly. *God, is this You?* Even so, the reality was that it was just a part-time position. Things would still be pretty tough for a while.

"You'd better call Mr. Phillips and see if he'll stop the eviction," Tasia told Ernie. Ernie had to step up to the plate. *If You're in this, Lord, it will all work out.*

Ernie reached for the telephone, the first call he'd initiated in months. The landlord was home and, surprisingly, agreed to accept a minimum payment schedule until they could catch up on their rent. More importantly, he agreed to call off the eviction.

God's fingerprints were showing up everywhere now. Within a time span of less than fifteen minutes, a seemingly impossible situation had been turned around. God *was* trustworthy; He *was* faithful; His word *was* true. Ah, but matters of the heart - in particular, hers and Ernie's relationship - would require more than just fifteen minutes to salvage, *if* there was anything that could be salvaged.

"I'm sorry for doubting you, Lord," Tasia whispered in the quiet of the kitchen. "Please forgive my hardness of heart."

Ernie had already left the room and slumped back in his usual place on the couch, but this time he shut off the television.

That night as Tasia and Ernie lay in bed, Tasia knew she couldn't keep up this façade much longer. In some ways, it might have been easier if the eviction *had* happened. Then she could feel somewhat justified in leaving Ernie. But now, everything had been turned around.

Lord, this is impossible, she prayed silently in the darkness of the bedroom. She scooted over as far as possible to her edge of the bed and turned on her side, her back to Ernie. *I don't love him-there's nothing left.*

Instantly, words came into Tasia's mind, as if someone were talking to her. *And just who do you think you are? When I died on the cross for you, there was nothing appealing about you. You were covered in sin, unaware that I protected you. But I loved you and you responded to My love. I love Ernie just as much as I love you. Allow Me to love him though you.*

Then, Lord, You'll have to do that, too! The words formed silently in her mind. *I know You love Ernie, but I can't do this on my own. It's in Your hands.* As she once again turned control over to Him, a peace settled into Tasia's heart, the first sense of peace she'd experienced in a long time. She drifted off into a restful sleep.

Tuesday morning, Tasia prepared breakfast as the kids assembled around the kitchen table. Ernie walked in just as she was putting out their bowls of cereal.

"Good morning," she said. The words came out of Tasia's mouth before she even realized what she'd said.

Ernie looked up at her, his head slightly tilted to the side and his jaw slack.

She hadn't planned on saying anything. Well, whatever. The words were out now.

"Good morning," he responded, cautiously taking his seat at the table.

Tasia handed him his bowl. Another change. This time, Ernie didn't retreat into the living room with his food.

"How are you?" Again, unplanned words came out of her mouth.

"Okay-and you?"

"All right." Boy, this was getting stranger by the minute.

Word by word, step by step, a relationship was in the process of being rebuilt. And so it continued, slowly but steadily with the passage of each new day. By the end of the week their communication became less stiff, their conversation flowing more freely.

The words of that one evening reverberated through Tasia's

consciousness whenever she felt like throwing in the towel. *Just what would make me think that I was any more special to God than Ernie?* She definitely was just as human as he.

Then came the first kiss, initiated by Ernie, on her cheek. Just a short kiss, the kind that says, "I care." Surprisingly, Tasia wasn't repulsed. She kissed him back in like fashion, timidly, sweetly.

Brick by brick, the wall that had built up between them slowly came down. In its place, a resolve to love was being cemented; a deeper commitment to each other emerged from the rubble of circumstances they'd come through.

Eventually, inevitably, Tasia's feelings followed suit. The chasm that had grown so wide between them in bed also began to shrink. Gradually, she accepted his touch. One night, Ernie reached over and held her, ever so tenderly, until they both fell asleep. He was sensitive to her, never pushing beyond what he felt she could emotionally accept, while her respect for him was rebuilding.

When they did physically join together again, Tasia was ready, willing, and able. She felt like a young bride again on her wedding night. In joyful expectancy, she took in the potency of his strong masculinity and completed it in ecstatic tenderness.

By autumn, their marriage was on solid footing again, stronger than ever, refined and forged in the fire of unconditional love.

Each path will lead somewhere
With distinct destinations –
Will you follow the crowd
Or your own inclinations?

✂ CHAPTER 22 ✂

Unconditional love – the highest form of love – the kind of love that sent Jesus to the cross – the kind of love that makes a marriage. Could she ever love that way again? The piercing ring of the telephone broke her reverie.

"Hi, Tasia? It's Carol. How's your week going?"

"Oh, hi, Carol. I've been pretty busy preparing for parent-teacher conferences. How's your business going?"

"It's been a good week. Got two new accounts so far and might close another insurance deal before the week's over. Hey, Tasia, if you haven't made plans yet for Saturday night, I was thinking of getting some of the girls together and going out dancing at Cadillac Ranch. Whad'ya think?"

"Sounds like it'd be fun. Is it 'girls only' or shall I invite Kurt, too?"

"That's entirely up to you, Tasia."

"Well, sounds like it'd be fun. I don't know if Kurt's got other plans or not, but I know he likes to kick up his heels, too. I'll get back to you, okay?"

"Sure, thing, Tasia. If I'm not here, just leave me a voicemail message. If you can make it, we'll meet you there at 7:30, okay? Catch you later."

"Okay, Carol. Thanks for the call."

As soon as she hung up with Carol, Tasia called Kurt.

"Tasia, I'd love to go with you, but I have a meeting that night with some of the other managers, remember?"

"Oh, that's right, I forgot. It would've been fun, but I understand. Maybe I should just stay home."

"Oh no, you don't. After the week you've had, I'll bet you could use some time out with your friends. You go on. Why don't we plan on going dancing next week?"

"All right – better get my dancin' shoes ready."

"Good. As for Sunday, shall I pick you up in time for Sunday School?"

"Yeah, that'd be good – about 8:30?"

"All right. Maybe later on, we could go to dinner and catch a show? I promise I won't keep you out late, not with class the next morning. In fact, why don't you pick the restaurant?"

"Oooh, now that's livin' dangerously," Tasia laughed. "All right, Kurt, you've got yourself a date."

"Tasia, the only *livin'* I want to do is with you – it'd only be *dangerous* otherwise!"

She could just picture his baby blues twinkling at the other end. She smiled at the thought. "Okay, you sweet talker, you. See ya Sunday. Good night."

"Good night, Tasia."

Tasia hung up and redialed Carol. Her voicemail answered. "Hi, Carol, this is Tasia. Kurt's got a meeting to attend, so it'll be girls' night out. I'll meet you over there at 7:30. See ya then."

By the time Tasia pulled into the parking lot, there were only a few parking spaces left. Carol, Marcia and Robin were waiting in the vestibule for her. They all hugged like jubilant adolescents.

"Hope you guys haven't been waiting too long," Tasia shouted over the loud beat.

"No, just got here a few minutes ago ourselves," Carol shouted back, scanning the crowd. "Looks like the place is hoppin'! Okay, girls – shall we?"

"Let's go!"

They jostled their way through the crowd and miraculously found an empty table toward the back of the room.

As they were taking off their coats, Tasia moistened her lips. "Boy, I'm thirsty. How 'bout the rest of you?"

"They serve Coke at the counter," Carol said. "Everyone for some Coke?"

They all nodded. "Good, it's unanimous. Why don't two of you stay here and guard the table while another comes with me to get the pop?" Tasia suggested.

"I'll come," volunteered Robin.

When they returned with the drinks, two guys were sitting at their table conversing with Carol and Marcia.

Tasia pretended to clear her throat. "Uh-hem."

The guys looked up and moved. "Sorry, ladies, didn't mean to take your spots." Looking back toward Carol and Marcia, they asked for the next dance.

Tasia watched the couples as they moved in rhythm to the music. Next thing she knew, Robin was out on the floor, too. It had been years since Tasia had been to a dance. She studied the movements of their steps, the motions of their bodies. Soon her body was swaying with the beat, too.

"Care to dance?"

Tasia pulled her eyes away from the crowd and looked up at a tall, handsome, dark-haired man. She guessed him to be right around her age. She glanced at his left hand. No ring. "Okay, but I better warn you – I'm pretty rusty!"

"Well, then, we'll just take it nice and slow." He smiled and continued, "My name's Ed." He reached out to take her by the hand.

"Hi, Ed. I'm Tasia." She accepted and followed him onto the dance floor. The first dance was a fast dance. Gradually, she felt her body loosening and moving with the beat. The second dance was a swing. Ed was true to his word. He guided her through it, though she felt a bit awkward and stepped on his toes more than once. The third dance was a slow dance. Ed held her close, stroking her long hair and eventually laid his hand against the small of her back. Tasia tried to relax against his body, but something just didn't feel right. She looked up at his face as he hummed the melody. His deep brown eyes searched her face. What did he see? Could he see into her soul? Could he sense her inner turmoil?

"Tasia, has anyone ever told you how beautiful you are?" His hands moved slightly lower on her back.

Tasia grimaced. "Ed, you seem like a nice guy, but I'm not here as a pick-up. I just came along with my friends 'cause my boyfriend couldn't make it out tonight."

"Well, then, it's his loss. If you were my girl, I wouldn't let you out of my sight." He pulled her in closer against his body.

Tasia's body straightened against his grip. "Guess that's the difference then between you two. He's not the controlling, pushy type." Tasia stopped and reached behind to move his hand away. "Thanks for the dance, Ed, but I think I've had enough." She turned and walked through the crowd till she found her friends back at the table.

"Girls, I've got to go."

"What happened, Tasia? It looked like you and that guy made a good dance pair," Robin said.

"Well, looks can be deceiving. This just doesn't feel right. I'll talk to you girls later." She grabbed her coat and purse, making a beeline to the exit. The three girls looked at each other and shrugged.

The next morning, the doorbell rang at 8:30. Tasia answered the door. "Hi, Kurt. Good to see you." She welcomed him with a warm hug.

Kurt returned the hug and swung her around. "So, how's m'lady today?"

"Oh, much better now," Tasia said as she studied Kurt's face. True, he was several years older than she; between his beard and mustache, he had more facial hair than on his head. But his strength and energy could rival someone ten years younger, and his heart was gentle and kind. And he loved the Lord.

"All right, then – let's get this show on the road." He caught her gaze and reached for her hand. "Tasia – are you all right?"

"Sure, Kurt, why do you ask?"

"I feel like I'm under a microscope. You haven't stopped looking at me since I got here." He chuckled in his light-hearted, warming way.

"Have I ever told you how handsome you are, Kurt?" Tasia lifted his hand to her face and slid it across her cheek. "You're a kind, gentle man, and I appreciate how freeing our relationship is."

Kurt looked like he'd just won a prize. His face relaxed, his eyes softened, as he gazed back at her. "Tasia, all I know is that I love you. If you feel free with me, it's because you've freed me, too." He took hold of her two hands and placed them together, palm-side up as if loosely cupping a large pearl of great price, and kissed her gently. "I think it's best that we go now," he suggested.

Tasia could feel her cheeks growing warm. "Yeah, I guess so."

Kurt helped her on with her coat and held the door open for her. "Ready?"

Sundays were special days for Tasia. She enjoyed her discussions with the kids in her Sunday School class. And Ernie's presence enriched it. Today's topic was God's unconditional love. How appropriate. The day passed quickly. Dinner was delicious and they enjoyed the movie. Tasia stayed nestled under Ernie's arm throughout most of it. On the way home, he asked, "So, how was the dance last night?"

Tasia put her hand on top of his knee. "Not that great, Kurt. I wound up leaving early."

"Really?" Kurt glanced at her. "Didn't you feel well?"

"Guess that depends on who was doing the feeling." She patted his knee nervously.

Kurt did a double-take. His bushy eyebrows furled forming a silent question.

"Don't worry, I'm all right, Kurt. It just didn't feel right dancing with anybody else." She looked at him and smiled. "I guess you've spoiled me."

Kurt pulled up into her driveway and looked back at her. "Well, then, I guess you'll just have to get used to it."

He walked around the car and opened her door. As they walked to her front door, he looked into her sleepy eyes. "Good night, Tasia." He hugged her and kissed her sweetly.

"Good night, Kurt," she said. Her eyelids were so heavy, drooping over her eyes. As she closed the door behind her and looked down, she noticed something glistening on her right hand. On her fourth finger was the ring Ernie had given her several years earlier – her 'God is Faithful' ring. Its diamond setting sparkled against the dim light. She smiled.

Previous flights had dead-ended
In her quest for something more –
Battered wings told of battles
Evidencing previous wars.

❧ CHAPTER 23 ❧

Life with Ernie began to settle down as the children grew up. Nights and weekends were usually filled with Josh's baseball and Lizzie's softball games and practices. In addition to everything else, she and Ernie were both actively involved with their teams. Ernie managed and Tasia was scorekeeper for Josh's Little League team. She also helped coach Lizzie's softball team. Besides sports, their children both took an interest in music, much to Tasia's delight. Josh preferred the sax; Lizzie the clarinet. There were music lessons to drive to, band practices, and school concerts to attend. Now in high school with interests of his own, Pete's involvement with the family centered mostly around dinnertime conversations. Financially, things improved and the couple started saving for a house-dreaming, setting goals, and working toward attaining those goals. Ernie, once again, proved to be a capable provider, an involved father, and a devoted husband.

One Sunday afternoon while Ernie and Tasia were out shopping, he drew her aside. "Honey, we've been through so much together. I want to give you something tangible as an expression of my love for you."

He walked her over toward the jewelry counter at Montgomery Wards; specifically, to the diamond ring section. The rings were on sale – fifty percent off – her kind of price. Since the day she had lost her wedding ring when she had been pregnant with Lizzie, she had been wearing a cheap band that she bought from a discount catalog. Even now, ten years later, she could vividly remember every painful detail of the day she lost her ring at the ice cream shop.

"Oh, Honey, that would be so nice."

"Okay then, Hon, pick out one that you like."

Tasia studied the selection on display. Her hands were perspiring, her pulse quickening. This was actually happening. Whatever ring she picked, it would have to be special – something symbolic of their marriage. *Lord,* Tasia prayed, *which one?* They all looked so beautiful. Then one caught her eye. Its setting held a round stone, almost like a flower or a star, with three diamond sprays trailing from it. Not only was the design different from the usual array, it immediately reminded her of the Trinity. The three diamond petals lay over a matching gold band, as if symbolically covering over their marriage. Her wedding ring set. Every time she looked at it, it would be a tangible reminder to her of God's great faithfulness.

Ernie smiled lovingly at his wife, so pleased to be able to bring such delight to the woman who so loved him. And to think she had once been ready to throw it all away.

The years passed quickly with ever-increasing love, moving closer to realizing goals. Pete's teenage years manifested the turbulence of his earlier childhood. His emotional problems affected every area of his life, as well as the lives of those around him. He seemed determined to alienate himself from everyone. Ernie didn't believe in professional counseling, so Tasia tried to reach Pete as best she could.

One summer day when she and Pete were the only ones at home, she confronted him. He sat on his bed, reading a paperback. Tasia pulled alongside him and sat on the edge of the mattress. "Pete, why are you so mean to Josh and Lizzie?"

Pete glared back at her, his brown eyes swirling with emotion. Was that anger she saw?

She pressed on. "Heck, you treated Pandy, our cat, better than you treat your own brother and sister."

He turned away.

She took him by his narrow shoulders and carefully turned him so he was facing her. "Pete, I know something's bothering you. Why do you have so much anger inside?"

Pete's pimply face turned red with emotion. "Wouldn't you, too, if *you* were kidnapped from *your* mother?"

"*Kidnapped?*" Memories of that terrible day so many years ago poured into Tasia's mind. What she had not been able to communicate to Pete then, she now felt free to explain. "Pete, tell me what you remember."

"I don't remember a lot, but I do remember you pulling me away from my mother and her crying out 'You're taking my child away from me!' How could you do that?" Pete glared at her, his wide eyes flashing defiantly. "Why did you have to mess up my life?"

"Come with me, Pete. You need to see something." Tasia reached for his hand, but he pulled it away. "Come with *me*," she reiterated, and this time she led the way into her bedroom. There she opened a file box and pulled out the folder that read 'Custody.' She found the form that Barbara had signed and handed it to Pete.

"Despite the show Barbara put on that afternoon, she told us she *wanted* us to raise you and *willingly* signed this change-of-custody order. I *never* kidnapped you."

Pete scanned the paper carefully. Tears filled his round eyes, until they spilled over.

Tasia reached out to hug him. "You need to know we love you. We would never do anything to intentionally hurt you."

He hugged her back.

Please, Lord, let that be it, she prayed.

But as soon as he turned eighteen, Pete moved out of the apartment to live with some friends Ernie and Tasia barely knew. The first dinner without him around the table seemed surreal.

"It's just so strange without Pete," Tasia finally said. "It's like this isn't even real."

Ernie drank a sip of his hot coffee. "Well, it was his decision to go."

"And I'm glad he's gone," said Josh. He glanced at Lizzie and took a bite of meatloaf.

Lizzie nodded in return. "I for one will sleep much easier now." She cut her meatloaf into pieces with her knife.

Tasia looked at Josh, then Lizzie, then back at Ernie. What were they talking about?

"So, dad, after dinner, do you think you can take me to the batting cages?" Josh asked.

"Depends on whether your homework's done," Ernie replied matter-of-factly.

Their home took on a more comfortable atmosphere, but Tasia knew from first-hand experience what a hard, unforgiving place the world could be. *Father, take care of him. Bring him to the point he needs to be in You,* became her prayer.

Tasia got a job at a local elementary school and loved working with the children. With the encouragement of her family, she started attending classes at Northeastern University, working toward a teaching degree. In addition to her new responsibilities, taking the time to operate her cleaning business proved challenging, but was necessary to help meet their rising expenses.

Lizzie's ten-year birthday was fast approaching. As Tasia and Lizzie drove through the neighborhood one Saturday afternoon on their way back from getting last-minute odds and ends for her birthday party, Lizzie pointed out a corner house with a 'For Sale' sign on the lawn. Tasia memorized the number and when they returned home, she called the realtor.

"I'm sorry, Ma'am, that house is already under contract," the realtor said. "However, I have *another* one that just came on the market that's just about a block away. I haven't even put the 'For Sale' sign up yet. If you're interested, I can show it to you."

Tasia mentioned it to Ernie and they agreed to check it out. The blond-brick bungalow had tall bushes under the front windows and a large, overgrown blue spruce in the front yard. When they entered the house, an uncomfortable feeling settled in the pit of Tasia's stomach. She paused and looked around.

Ernie studied her face. "Honey, what's wrong?"

"I'm not sure – can't quite put my finger on it. Oh well, let's see the rest of the place."

The realtor explained that the owner, an elderly woman, had already moved out. The house was clean enough. But something about the place just didn't feel right.

It would need some work, particularly new coats of a lighter paint to brighten up the olive-drab rooms, but no major repairs were necessary and the cost was in their ballpark. With a living room, kitchen, three bedrooms, a bathroom, full-size basement, and detached two-car garage, as well as a large rectangular-shaped backyard, it seemed like a dream come true.

Later, out of the realtor's hearing, they dismissed Tasia's concern as the result of the depressing colors inside. Two months later, they closed and moved into their new home, so much larger and more spacious than the little apartment their family of five had lived in for the past ten years.

"So, you're the new neighbor," said the dark-haired lady next door as she introduced herself to Tasia. The wind tossed a spray of water from her hose onto Tasia as she continued watering her bushes beneath the front windows. "My name's Sonja." She was about Tasia's height, maybe in her early thirties, and spoke with a heavy Ukrainian accent.

"Nice to meet you, Sonja. I'm Tasia. Say, what can you tell me about this house's previous owner?"

"Guess you don't know the story about this place then. Old man Darby was killed around here about a year ago."

Tasia rubbed the side of her head and looked at the tree-lined street. She did indeed remember Mr. Darby. Every morning, she would see him faithfully go for his daily walk past their apartment. Then she didn't see him for a while. Neighborhood gossip said that his fifty-plus-year-old girlfriend had suffocated him with a pillow because she thought she was pregnant. She wasn't; it was probably just hormonal tricks that can accompany that age. In any event, she had been found not guilty by reason of insanity and was now safely tucked away in a state-run mental institution.

"Well," Sonja continued, "this was her mother's house. She used to live in the back bedroom. Boy, the stories I could tell you."

Tasia wanted to hear more, but a dark-haired young boy's head poked out the front door and called to Sonja.

"That's my son, Adam. I'll catch up with you next time," she called over her shoulder as she walked back toward her house.

Maybe that had something to do with the strange feeling she'd experienced the first time they walked inside the house. Had a sinister spiritual presence lingered after its former residents left? Or had the former residents fallen victim to unseen antagonists already present within the house?

What happens in the spiritual realm
Is manifest in natural surroundings;
But Satan makes counterfeit copies
Of God's great love abounding.

❈ CHAPTER 24 ❈

After they moved in, things settled down. How much stuff they had accumulated over the years!

With a little free time on her hands, one day while the kids were at school and Ernie was at work she baked a treat for the family. Brownies, one of their favorites. She could tell by the rich, chocolaty aroma filling the room that the brownies must be ready, even though the timer showed a few more minutes left to go. As she bent over the oven and pulled them out, she had the definite feeling that someone was behind her. Tasia pivoted, but didn't see anyone. An eerie feeling engulfed her, one that she didn't like at all.

Tasia commanded, "Any presence that is in this house that is not of God, leave now by the authority of the Name of the Lord Jesus."

A sense of peace filled her spirit. If there was anything there before, it was gone now.

A few weeks later, while having breakfast around the kitchen table, Josh asked his dad why he had been up so late working downstairs in the basement. "I heard you using your paper cutter. It woke me up and I had a hard time getting back to sleep."

Lizzie chimed in, "Yeah, me too."

"I haven't been working down in the basement at night," Ernie replied, one bushy eyebrow slightly upraised. He looked at Tasia.

"Me, either," Tasia responded.

Josh shrugged. "Well, *somebody* has."

Ernie waved his hand. "There must be some other explanation. Maybe you just heard strange sounds coming from the furnace that you're not used to hearing." He got up to refill his coffee cup, returned to the table and lit a cigarette. "So, what's on today's schedule?" he asked.

Tasia, however, made a point to talk to the kids further about it in private. She wasn't so sure that it should be so easily dismissed, especially after what she had experienced in the kitchen some weeks earlier. She and Ernie had come to an understanding that any "spiritual stuff" would be done on her own time, without him around, and she stuck to it.

Before saying goodnight to Josh and Lizzie, Tasia sat down on Josh's bed, with the two of them taking their usual positions alongside her. "Do you remember the sounds you said you heard at night?"

They both nodded.

"Whether the paper cutter was actually making slicing sounds the other night, or there's some other explanation for the sounds you heard, I think it's important that you know what your rights are as children of God," Tasia said, putting her arms reassuringly around them. Both Josh and Lizzie had made professions of faith in Jesus as their savior a few years earlier.

"Once when I was down in the basement by the furnace room, it felt like someone had put their hand on my shoulder," Lizzie said, her hazel eyes opening wide. "But when I turned around, nobody was there."

"How come you didn't tell me?" Tasia asked, swallowing her shock. She ran her hand soothingly over Lizzie's thick hair. "It's okay, Lizzie. So, what did you do then?"

"I ran upstairs and out into the backyard as fast as I could," Lizzie replied, scooting closer to Tasia.

"Well, next time you sense something weird around you, tell it to *be gone in Jesus' name*," Tasia told them. Then she relayed her incident in the kitchen, and how she commanded the presence to leave. Tasia paused and looked first at Josh, then at Lizzie before continuing. "To pray in the name of Jesus is to ask for or claim the things which His blood has secured for you. So, if you ever come across something that scares you, like what some people call ghosts or demons, and you know it isn't from God, you have the authority to speak in Jesus' name and command it to go away." She got up from the bed and knelt on the floor in front of them.

"It's nothing you need to be afraid of," Tasia stressed. Then she took hold of Josh and Lizzie's hands and prayed over them, thanking God for His love and praying His protection over them so that they would have a peaceful sleep and wake up refreshed, ready for the new day. And just to reinforce their conversation, she commanded any evil spirits in the house to be gone, in Jesus' name.

Tasia switched off their lights and softly walked away to her own bedroom. Many good years were spent in that house, besides the need for an occasional 'spiritual cleaning.'

The front doorbell rang one crisp sunny Saturday afternoon in the fall. Ernie answered the door with Tasia close behind. A tall man dressed in a trench coat showed him his ID card. "I'm Agent Nurello from the FBI and I have some important information for you,"

The agent informed them that the previous owner's daughter, Ernestine, who had been tried earlier for the first-degree murder of her boyfriend and found not guilty by reason of insanity, had escaped from the state's mental institution. "Unfortunately," he continued, "she escaped yesterday and we suspect that she might try to find her way back to her old home."

Tasia gasped and stepped back. This sounded more like a scene out of a soap opera than real life.

Ernie uncharacteristically put his arm around Tasia, his gaze never leaving the agent.

"This is a picture of Ernestine. If she comes here, do not open your door to her. Instead, immediately call the number on this sheet of paper. We'll take it from there. If you have anybody else living here, make sure they understand the seriousness of this matter."

Ernie thanked the agent and moments later explained the situation to Josh and Lizzie, a very unsettling experience for them all.

The next afternoon, Ernie took the kids for a ride and returned home carrying a four-month-old Labrador Retriever in his arms. Josh ran ahead and opened the back door. The puppy was quivering. Its large honey-brown eyes looked up pitifully at Tasia. Poor thing! It was just as cute as it could be. Its body was disproportionate in size, kind of like an adolescent whose body parts grow awkwardly at different rates, and its oversized paws and large floppy ears were indicators of size to come.

The dog needed a name. After hearing everyone's suggestions, they decided on Lizzie's selection, "Hershey." Hershey became a loving, welcome addition to the Franklin family. He had found a home.

Tasia answered the telephone later that evening. "Sorry to bother you, Ma'am. This is Agent Nurello from the FBI. I have some good news for you and your family. Ernestine was picked up hitchhiking today on the Northwest Tollway. She's been returned to the mental institution. Well, enjoy the rest of your evening." Tasia hung up the phone and looked at Josh and Lizzie playing on the floor with Hershey.

Ernie sat on the couch reading the paper. He lowered it and asked, "Who was that on the phone?"

"That FBI agent. He said they picked Ernestine up hitchhiking today on the Northwest Tollway and returned her to the mental institution."

"Northwest Tollway? You mean Route 90? Honey, that expressway runs a path straight from the mental institution to here!" Ernie exhaled and stubbed his cigarette out in the ashtray.

Ernie grew restless with his job as a body-shop manager. When an acquaintance offered him a position as a staff appraiser for an independent auto-appraisal company, with Ernie's thorough knowledge of cars, it seemed the perfect job. The added benefit of working on a computer at home gave him the flexibility to work around the family's busy schedules.

Finally the day came – Tasia graduated, with honors. Now all she needed was a job, but the market was already flooded with teachers. Tasia saturated the nearby school districts with her resume and finally accepted a job teaching third grade in a local elementary school. Who would have ever imagined!

Since all truth is parallel
And God's great love infinite –
His mercy is unending,
His faithfulness knows no limit.

○3 CHAPTER 25 ♂○

One Saturday afternoon, while Tasia was down in the basement working on some school papers, the telephone rang upstairs. She ran up the stairs and grabbed the receiver off the wall phone in the kitchen. "Hello, Franklin residence."

"Hello, Mom?"

Oh Lord, could it be? Tasia sat down on the oak bench, part of the kitchen nook set, her tired legs ready to give out. "Pete?" Her breathless voice sounded foreign to her own ears. "Pete, is that you?"

"Hi, Mom, how are you?" His voice had a deeper, more mature sound to it than she remembered.

"Fine. Pete, are you okay? We've missed you!" They had already run through the gamut of emotions regarding his abrupt departure and his lack of communication. They had tried to reach him, but to no avail. Lately, whenever she raised his name in prayerful concern, the words 'son of disobedience' shot across her mind. There were so many questions she wanted to ask him, but didn't want to throw them at him all at once.

"Yeah, I'm okay. I've missed you, too…How's Dad and the kids?"

"Everyone's doing fine. Pete, where are you?" Had his appearance changed any over the past few years?

"I've got an apartment in Streamwood. Things are going all right."

She had hoped to hear a more enthusiastic response in his voice. "Good, Pete, glad to hear it. Did you know we've moved since you left? We were able to keep the same phone number, though, 'cause we're in the same neighborhood. Maybe you could come by for a visit?" Tasia offered.

"Yeah...maybe. Anybody else around?"

"No, your dad's not home right now, and Josh and Lizzie are at band practice." She still couldn't get over it – she hadn't known if she would *ever* talk to him again. "It's so good to hear your voice, Pete. Is there a number we can reach you at?"

"No, I don't have one yet. I'm on a public phone right now, so don't have much time to talk. Well, give them my love."

That was it? There was so much more she wanted to say. "All right," she said instead, adding, "Pete, one more thing before you go. Promise me you'll keep in touch, okay?"

"Okay, Mom. Well, I'd better go now. Love you."

"We love you too, Pete."

Thank God he was all right. True to his word, every now and then Pete would call to keep in touch, but for whatever reasons, he still chose to keep his distance.

Both Josh and Lizzie now attended the same high school, separated only by a couple of years. Josh would graduate in the spring.

Josh admired his dad and although he was offered a college scholarship, his interests leaned more toward the trades. Ernie would have preferred to see Josh go into another field, but Josh could not be dissuaded.

"One thing I want you to promise me, Josh – don't become an auto mechanic, all right?"

"All right, Dad. I promise."

Following Josh's high school graduation, Ernie began grooming Josh for the automotive field, a special time for the father and son pair, doing the "male bonding" thing.

Even Lizzie's relationship with her dad had changed. No longer a little girl, yet always 'Daddy's little girl,' Ernie opened up more of his life to her, relaxing a little on the parental side and revealing more of his human side.

One summer day when Tasia got home, Ernie was lying on the couch, just staring up at the ceiling. This wasn't typical behavior for him, so she went over to him, bent down, and gave him a gentle kiss.

"Are you okay, Honey?"

He looked up at her, his dark brown eyes wide open, his mouth drawn in a straight line. "You almost lost me today."

Tasia's eyebrows pressed together, her smooth forehead now wrinkled in concerned lines.

Ernie explained how a truck had smashed into the passenger side of his car and catapulted it into the middle of a busy intersection just as the light changed and traffic charged ahead. "I can't believe I'm even alive. You should've seen the car – it's completely totaled!"

"Thank God you're all right!" Tasia exclaimed, examining him quickly for any signs of injury. Everyone must eventually die, but the reality that Ernie's life could be snuffed out in just a moment's time hadn't really sunk in before.

Satisfied that he appeared to be okay, she said, "I think God's trying to get your attention, Honey. I guess He's not done with you yet," she half-joked.

Ernie laughed and pulled her close. "Well then, I guess that's a good thing."

Loving eyes and tender lips,
Compassionate and strong –
Peacefulness enfolds me
When I'm wrapped inside your arms.

☙ CHAPTER 26 ❧

Ernie and Tasia began preparing Josh and Lizzie for their next phase of life – independence from their parents. More and more, Tasia heard Ernie reinforce the idea.

One Sunday afternoon, a unusually warm day for early September, Josh and Lizzie were outside shooting baskets. Josh wore a Bulls t-shirt and blue jean cut-offs; Lizzie wore her oversized Bears t-shirt and had her hair in short pigtails. Ernie, donned in jeans and a casual button-down shirt, joined them. Never one to be left on the sidelines, Hershey got in on the action, too, running interference between their legs. When they had enough, they all sat down on the grass, exhausted. Hershey lay panting at Ernie's side.

"Josh, Lizzie, there's going to be a lot of changes in our lives over the next few years. Pete's already on his own. Josh, soon you'll be, too, and Lizzie, you'll be going off to college. You need to know that as brother and sister, you'll always share a very close bond with each other, no matter what you do with your lives. And your mom and I need to start preparing for the day when you'll both be on your own."

Josh lay down in the grass, his hands tucked under his head. "Gee, Dad, you make it sound so serious."

"It's just a reality of life, Josh," Ernie replied, petting Hershey who was now finally catching his breath.

Lizzie had placed her applications with various colleges and finally settled on Winona State University in Michigan. After a weekend excursion with the family to check it out, she received her parent's blessings.

Josh was busy working at a local branch of First National Bank, trying to save money for the day he would get his own apartment.

Soon, Tasia and Ernie would be empty nesters, a difficult time of adjustment for many couples.

After Tasia cleared away the dinner dishes one weekday evening, she and Ernie sat at the kitchen table having a cup of coffee together. Tasia mentioned her concerns to Ernie. "Honey, are we going to be okay – you know, as a couple – once the kids are gone?"

"Tell you what, Hon, why don't you keep next Sunday open for just you and me," Ernie said.

"And just what have you got up your sleeve?" Tasia asked slyly.

"Oh, you'll see," Ernie said, his dark brown eyes twinkling.

That next Sunday morning, he and Tasia said goodbye to the kids as they got into their car. "I'm taking your mom for a ride," Ernie explained. "Probably won't be back 'til dinnertime. See you then." And off they drove.

The day was sunny, with just a slight touch of coolness in the breeze – perfect for a ride. Nature had just begun to don its autumn dress; its leaves were seasoned in softly tinged pale yellows and wisps of red. Quaint farmhouses and picturesque barns flavored the rolling landscape. The ride through the countryside was a visual feast.

Ernie knew that Tasia loved being outdoors in nature. One of her favorite places was Starved Rock, but years had passed since she'd last been there.

When Tasia finally saw the road sign and realized their destination, she clasped her hands together with delight. "Honey, I don't believe it! This is great!"

Ernie parked in the gravel lot and they began to hike, something they hadn't done together in years. Following along an ascending trail, they came upon a small clearing at the edge of a steep drop-off and stopped for a breather on a nearby log. Ernie got out of breath more frequently than he used to, something he attributed to smoking and the 'aging process.'

"Honey, I want you to know that you are the most important person in my life," he said, looking at his bride of the past twenty-two years. Aside from a few gray hairs, her brown curly hair was as lustrous as the day he first saw her. He took hold of her hand. "Pete's on his own, soon Josh will be moving out, and Lizzie will be away at college. Tasia, I want you to know how much I love you. Now we can start doing things and working toward goals for just the two of us."

"Sounds like you've got something in mind."

"Maybe…yeah, actually, a few ideas. Whad'ya think of the idea of buying a mobile home and traveling to different parts of the country for vacations? Or we could buy a piece of land up north and build a summer cottage. Tasia, the possibilities are endless and the best is yet to come."

She looked lovingly at Ernie; his dark eyes were bright and full of life. His full head of black hair was just slightly receding above his temples. A few extra pounds had settled around his midsection, but his heart had stayed true to her over all these years. She truly loved this man, her husband, and father of her children. Tasia felt like they were starting out all over again, dreaming and making plans for the future, but this time much wiser.

Yes, life would inevitably change, but they would still have each other.

Released from what held it,
New adventures now beckon –
Cracks that need filling
For love's new dimension.

☙ CHAPTER 27 ❧

Thanksgiving was one of Tasia's favorite holidays. She had so much to be thankful for. Tasia's whole family came to spend Thanksgiving Day with them. Her brothers were all married now with families of their own, and her mom and dad were just a few years away from celebrating their fiftieth wedding anniversary. They always had a good time whenever they all got together to visit. The sound of young voices mingling with adult conversation, and the aroma of the feast filled the Franklin home.

Inevitably, Nature's autumn dress gave way to her frosty winter coat. Holiday preparations were in full swing with Christmas just a couple of weeks away. Perhaps next weekend they would all go out and find the perfect tree to decorate, a far cry from the one dollar Charlie Brown tree they bought that long-ago Christmas Eve.

Thursday came quickly. Tasia served dinner to her family waiting around the kitchen table. Dinnertime was always family time in the Franklin house, a special time of interaction when the day's events and feelings were shared with one another; world and community events were discussed; and opinions and ideas were offered, chewed, and digested, along with the rest of the meal.

Tasia always looked forward to that part of the day. Though she could preplan the meal, conversations around the kitchen table were always spontaneous and often lively, interwoven with each one's contributions like a colorful patchwork quilt. This particular evening was no different than any others.

When dinner was done, Josh was first to excuse himself to go out with some of his friends for the evening. "I won't be back too late," he called as he headed out the back door.

Not long afterward, Ernie mentioned he wasn't feeling well and left the table, walking down the hallway toward their bedroom. Though concerned, Tasia thought his discomfort was related to breathing problems Ernie had been experiencing lately. Forever the stubborn one when it came to doctors, Ernie had taken some over-the-counter medicine to relieve his intermittent wheezing, attributing it to a slight bronchial infection. She and Lizzie continued talking. About five minutes passed without Ernie returning to the kitchen.

Tasia gazed down the long hallway leading to their bedroom. An uneasiness gnawed at her. "I'll be right back, Lizzie. I'm going to go check on your dad."

Tasia entered the bedroom and her heart nearly stopped. Ernie stood by his bureau, holding his head in both his hands, supported by his elbows.

"Honey, are you okay? Is it another migraine?" Tasia asked softly, tiptoeing closer to his side.

"I don't know...I just don't feel right." He took several short breaths.

"Are you having trouble catching your breath? Do you want to go see a doctor?" she asked, placing her hand on Ernie's right shoulder.

"No, I'll come back and join you both in a moment," he said quietly, not turning his head. "I just need a few more minutes."

"Okay." Tasia ambled toward the kitchen and rejoined Lizzie, sharing what Ernie had said. Another five minutes passed before he rejoined them. Tasia quickly scanned his face. His normally ruddy-looking skin tone had turned ghastly pale.

Tasia stood and walked over to him. "Honey," she said in a firm tone, "I really think we should go to the hospital." She knew not to push him too hard, but this was not normal. As she reached out to touch his hand, its cold, clammy surface confirmed the need to go quickly.

"No, I'll be okay," Ernie insisted.

"Dad," Lizzie ordered, "you're going!" Lizzie grabbed his coat from the closet and together she and Tasia helped him put it on.

"Lizzie, you stay home in case Josh returns and let him know what's going on. As soon as I have any news, I'll call you," Tasia said, grabbing her coat and purse. She helped Ernie into the car.

The cold air hit Ernie like a ton of bricks, intensifying his already difficult breathing. In between taking short, rapid breaths, he said, "Honey — take me — to the fire — station instead. — I don't think — I'll make it—- to the — hospital."

Northwest Community Hospital was about a fifteen-minute drive from their house; the local fire station was just three blocks away. Tasia raced to the firehouse, leaving Ernie in the parked car with the motor and heat running, rang the doorbell and pounded her fist against the metal door.

Seconds seemed like an eternity. She glanced back toward the car. Ernie was still struggling to breathe. "Lord, please bring someone quickly!"

A paramedic answered the door. Tasia quickly explained the situation and showed him the box of medicine Ernie had taken.

He called out to another colleague and they sprang into action. As one pulled the ambulance out of the garage, the other wasted no time in securing Ernie on a gurney, quickly lifting him into the ambulance through its rear doors. Tasia climbed inside, too, and they were off to the hospital.

"What's your husband's age?"

"Fifty-three."

"How long ago did he take the medicine?"

"About an hour ago."

"Any allergies? History of heart trouble?"

"None."

By this time, Ernie was hyperventilating and gasping for breath. The paramedic placed a clear plastic breathing apparatus over Ernie's face, covering his mouth and nose. A cloudy white vapor fed through it for Ernie to inhale. He looked at her with eyes wide open in panic.

"What's that you're giving him to breathe?"

"It's to help calm his heart down – we have to try to slow his heart rate; it's racing too fast." Turning to Ernie, he instructed, "Now, breathe this in as deeply as you can."

Ernie tried to comply by taking deep breaths, but it was so hard for him to do. His heart was beating too rapidly.

The ambulance raced toward the hospital, its screaming sirens wailing. Time slowed to a crawl as Ernie fought for each minute of life.

She held his hand firmly. His grip was limp and clammy. She watched his chest rise and fall in dangerous rapid succession.

They pulled up to the emergency entrance at Northwest Community Hospital. The wide metal doors swung open and white-uniformed attendants rushed out. In a blur of motion, they transferred Ernie out of the ambulance and wheeled him into the emergency room.

Tasia followed, but was gently detoured into the waiting room. "Sorry, Ma'am, but you're not allowed in there. We'll let you know when there's any change."

Tasia watched helplessly as the doors closed behind the gurney, blocking her view of Ernie. *Father, please take care of him*, she prayed. *If ever he needed You, it's now.*

Tasia took a seat among the other people in the waiting room. She glanced at her watch: *7:30 p.m.* A little boy, probably not more than six, cried while his mother tried to comfort him. What could be wrong? Across the aisle, the expressionless faces of a young Latino couple stared at the television. Two seats down, a woman in a wheelchair with a cast on her leg slowly crunched on Doritos.

Tasia picked up a magazine, but the words jumbled together as her thoughts replayed the events of the past half-hour.

"Mrs. Franklin!"

Tasia snapped out of her reverie. She lifted her head and turned toward the direction of the voice. A slender nurse stood looking over the waiting assembly, her eyes scouring the room.

"Mrs. Franklin?" the young nurse called and made eye contact with Tasia, walking briskly, past the mother with the wailing child and the Latino couple.

"Yes?"

"The doctor wants you to know there's no change yet and that they're doing everything they possibly can for your husband. Come with me, you'll be more comfortable in this room," she said, leading

Tasia to a separate enclosure. "Is there anything I can get for you?"

"No thanks, I'll be fine."

"Maybe you'd like some company while you're waiting, perhaps a chaplain?"

Tasia took a long, slow breath and exhaled. *Patience.* "Thanks anyway, but I'll be all right."

The four walls enclosing her were painted a light blue, soothing to the eyes. A round table centered in the middle of the room had four dark-blue upholstered chairs positioned around it. Scenic paintings of majestic mountains and meandering streams mounted in plain wooden frames were hung on two adjacent walls. The scenes looked so tranquil, unlike the unrelenting nightmare that engulfed her and Ernie.

A few minutes later, a rotund, pleasant-looking man in his early forties entered the room. As their eyes met, his smile faded. "Mrs. Franklin, I'm Chaplain Mike Morris, a volunteer here at Northwest. Would you mind if I stayed a bit and visited with you?"

These people felt she needed company. Did she look that bad? What *was* going on with Ernie? "Be my guest, but it's really not necessary."

"Tell me what happened," he coaxed, gently sliding into the chair beside her.

Tasia relived the past brief moments for him, ending with: "But I'm sure Ernie will be fine." Then remembering his earlier accident in the summer, added, "He's had close swipes with death before. Funny," Tasia continued, "Ernie always said he didn't need Jesus in his life, that that was just for people who needed a crutch. Well, if ever he needed that 'Someone' in his life, it's now."

The room was silent for a while.

"Mind if I pray with you?" asked the chaplain in a low, comforting voice.

Tasia nodded.

"Father, You know what's going on here better than we do, and we know it's not Your will that anybody should perish but through your Son, Jesus, have eternal life. I pray for Ernie, Lord, for his salvation and Your protection over him. I pray for his family, too, that You strengthen them during this time. In Jesus' name, Amen."

"Amen," echoed Tasia. Connecting to God through prayer always helped lighten her burdens.

They talked about her family and the chaplain's family, how she came to know the Lord and how he did, including what had led him into a volunteer ministry at the hospital.

"God is love," the chaplain replied. "Some of the people in here hurt so badly. If I can share some of that love with them – be His instrument – then that's worth it."

Tasia glanced at the big round clock on the wall – 9 o'clock. Surely, they would hear something soon.

Someone knocked on the door and opened it. A middle-aged man in bright green scrubs walked toward her. She tried, unsuccessfully, to read his stoic expression. "How's he doing?"

The doctor's eyes cast downward. "We did everything we could. He had a strong heart; we just couldn't get it to slow down. It finally just gave out."

Tasia sat motionless. This couldn't be real. *God, how could this be happening?*

"I'm so sorry. Do you want to see him?"

The doctor and the chaplain led Tasia into the ER. There lay Ernie's still body – calm, finally. No more breathing ordeals, no more racing heart. She looked at Ernie's ashen face. His lustrous brown eyes were closed forevermore. She closed her own eyes, recalling his look of panic as he fought, panting for each breath. Then she looked for any indication of fear in his expression, but now only quiet calm covered his stately face.

Had Ernie accepted Jesus as his sin bearer? Had he made his peace with God while there was still time? That was the only hope Tasia had left to cling to. Would she see him again in eternity, or would this be her final goodbye? *Father, is he with You? I could bear all this as long as I know he's with You.*

Slowly, she bent over and softy kissed Ernie's forehead. The brush of her lips on his already unnaturally cool face brought tears to her eyes. She remembered the first time her lips had lightly touched his the evening of their second date. It would never be again. She would never see him again, this side of eternity. The form in front of her no longer held the essence of the man she knew and loved. "Goodbye, Ernie - I love you...." Her tears fell on his unfeeling face. Her throat constricted against the cries she desperately tried to hold back.

A hand lightly touched her shoulder, and only then was she aware of the other two people in the room. They had schedules to keep, other people to attend to. Time was so short. This was all so final. She wanted to remember everything about him: every smile, every touch, every hug. *I will remember you always, Ernie.*

This was all happening so fast – *too fast!* Her legs began to tremble. She felt weak – so terribly, intensely weak.

They helped walk her back to the enclosed room, supporting her by her arms.

"Is there anyone you can call to come pick you up?" Chaplain Mike asked.

Tasia couldn't think clearly. A thick, numbing fog had encased her mind – her very soul.

Lord, who can I call? Someone who lived close by and knew them well; someone who the kids trusted; someone who knew her heart.

The name of an old, dear friend came to mind who had lived with them in the same apartment building so many years before, who had also come to experience the Lord's love and healing touch upon her own life.

Her hands reached toward her purse for her address book. She tried to fumble through its pages, her hands shaking. Her eyes refused to focus through the thick encircling mist.

"Here, let me dial the number for you," Chaplain Mike said, as he reached for her address book.

Lord, please let them be home. The phone rang twice before someone answered it.

"Maggie, this is Tasia." Her tongue felt thick and uncooperative in her mouth, each word a deliberate chore. "Can you or Ron come pick me up from Northwest Community Hospital? Ernie's dead and I...." The words were foreign sounding even to her own ears.

"Tasia? Tasia, is that you?" the warm, caring voice asked on the other end. "We'll be right there. You just stay put." The phone line disconnected.

Tasia handed the telephone back to Chaplain Mike and asked him to dial her home next. "I have to tell Lizzie."

Lizzie answered on the first ring.

"Lizzie...." A wave of pain gripped her heart.

"I already know, Mom. Dad's dead, isn't he?"

"How did you know? Who told you?"

"No one. This evening, around 9 o'clock, I looked up at the clock and had the strangest feeling that Dad was gone." Her soft voice was saturated with emotion. "Are you okay, Mom?"

She had to be strong for them all. If this was that hard for her, what would it be like for the kids? She had to get a grip. "Maggie and Ron are coming to the hospital to bring me home. I need you to be there in case Josh comes back before I get there."

"All right, Mom. Be careful. I love you."

"I love you, too, Lizzie."

"Pete. I have to call Pete and let him know."

The helpful chaplain dialed his number and again handed her the phone. It rang and rang until finally the prompt came to leave a voicemail message. "Pete, this is Mom. I'm at the hospital. I brought Dad here because...of complications from some medicine he took." Should she tell him on the phone now or in person? He wasn't much good at returning calls. No, she couldn't chance it. This was not a time to play games. "Pete," she began, "Dad died tonight around 9:00 p.m. I'll be home a little later, so call when you get this message." It would hit him hard, but death is never delicate. She had no choice.

Who else? Her parents; Ernie's brothers. They could call all the other family members and relay the news.... Her thoughts became muddled; a murky veil covered her mind. She felt like she had just been smashed flat and left abandoned on the road. Time was a hazy blur. Nothing mattered anymore, except for the kids. At some point, her friends arrived at the hospital and took her home.

The rest of the night was an obscured haze. Someone must have borrowed her keys and driven the car back home from the fire station. Sometime after 10 o'clock, folks started coming over.

Around 11 o'clock, Josh entered through the back door of the house, hung up his coat and stared at all the people milling around in the kitchen. "What's going on?" he asked, surveying the unconventional scene.

Lizzie walked over toward him. Josh looked at her; then his gaze darted in Tasia's direction. Her eyes, too, were all puffy and red. He searched past all the people. "Dad? Where's Dad?" he asked. His open mouth and eyes wide in alarm displayed the inner struggle of uncertainty at not knowing, and the fearful dread of actually finding out.

"Josh," Tasia began, forcing words through her quivering lips, "Josh, Dad's gone."

"Gone?"

"Josh, Dad's dead." His mouth gaped open and his brown eyes flashed back at her in disbelief.

"He was having trouble breathing, Josh; his heart wouldn't slow down —."

"No." All eyes turned toward him. He searched their faces for signs of hope, but their straight-lined expressions and saddened eyes only confirmed her words.

"Noooooooo," he cried, running toward the front door without his coat. He burst into the frigid darkness, the anguish of his soul exploding into the stillness of the night. "Nooooooo!!!!!"

She listened, all her senses attuned to the moment – her very being ached with him – their cries joining in time and space. Nothing had prepared them for this. *Oh God, how could this be happening?*

It would do no good to go after him. Josh would have to deal with this terrible reality on his own terms.

Pete came over as soon as he got the message. Lizzie carefully went over every detail with him. Pete sat quietly by himself, as if deep in thought.

After awhile, Josh did return home, his eyes as red as his half-frozen skin. He slumped down in a kitchen chair, like an exhausted, defeated warrior. "How did it happen?" he asked bluntly.

Tasia explained the evening's events, beginning at the point when Josh had left after dinner that evening.

As the pieces slowly began to fit together, Josh let his tears flow.

All his dreams – gone! In an instant, *all* their worlds had collapsed. "What do I do now?" he asked, looking at Tasia for an answer – one that never came.

She had never felt so useless.

"We'll get through this, Mom. He'd want me to be strong." Around midnight, Josh thanked the rest of his relatives for coming. "We need to get some rest," he said protectively of his Mom and Lizzie. "I think we're all exhausted."

Pete lingered a bit longer after everyone else had long gone. There they sat around the kitchen table where just hours earlier the three of them talked and laughed while eating dinner together as a family.

"We'll have to make funeral arrangements tomorrow," Tasia said. Somehow she had to hold herself together and get through this. *Think - plans for tomorrow - calls to make.* Her head ached. She tried to think, but just couldn't.

Josh put his arm on Tasia's shoulder. "Come on, Mom, let's get some sleep. You need some rest."

Pete said he'd return in the morning to help make the funeral arrangements.

The thought of going back in the bedroom and lying down on *their* bed brought more tears to Tasia's eyes.

Lizzie's tender voice was soothing and kind. "I'll sleep with you, Mom. I'll keep you company."

They crawled into the bed, clothes and all. What was the sense of changing clothes, anyway? There just was no sense to any of this. She had been ripped apart in a moment's time. The darkness of the room paralleled the emptiness in her heart. She lay motionless on the bed for what seemed like hours, but was, in reality, only minutes.

"Mom, you're still crying?"

Tasia didn't think Lizzie was aware of her muffled sobs. Now *she* was keeping Lizzie from getting *her* needed rest. "I'm sorry, Lizzie...."

"Mom . . ." Lizzie rolled over and faced toward Tasia.

Tasia could dimly see the silhouette of her daughter's shoulder-length hair brushing against her slender shoulders in the darkness.

"Do you remember when I was a little girl and you used to sing to me? One of the songs was 'Jesus Loves Me,' remember?"

Tasia nodded. "Yes, but that was so long ago...."

Then her daughter sang to her, softly, in the midst of her *own* pain, trying to ease the pain of the one who had taught her: Jesus loves me, this I know, for the Bible tells me so..., (ending with) Yes, Jesus loves me. The Bible tells me so.

Tasia smiled through her tears. Roles had momentarily reversed. Daughter sang to mother; comfort received was now comfort given.

"Thank you, Lizzie, thanks for the reminder. I needed that," Tasia said softly as she leaned over and kissed her daughter on her forehead. "Now you get some rest, okay? Sleep with Jesus' angels."

"You, too, Mom," she said, drifting off to sleep.

Tasia lay on her back, staring into the blackness of the night. Lizzie was right – Tasia was not alone. She needed to turn the focus of her attention from the darkness of her despair back toward her loving Lord. Using all her resolve, she now willed her attention to the One who understood it all, defying her emotions.

No sooner had she done that, did Tasia feel as if all her burdens lifted from her. Whether her spirit had actually left her body or not, she couldn't tell. She just felt such peace encircle her; she felt so light. Then, an embrace. Not a flesh-to-flesh embrace, but an embrace, nonetheless. She sighed. Such a comforting embrace...then it was gone.

Where was she? She opened her eyes. She was in bed; there was Lizzie – and then she remembered why Lizzie was there instead of her beloved husband. *Oh, Ernie...* Instantly, the weight and sadness of the day washed all over her again.

No, she would not despair. Now she knew she had a choice, even in this. She was not alone. The Lord was so close to her. Tasia again turned her focus toward Him. Again, she experienced the same freeing sensation of being lifted up out of her heaviness – again the comforting embrace – ah, how sweet His presence!

This time when her awareness returned, Tasia kept her focus on the Lord. It didn't change the reality of the day's events, but she knew beyond a shadow of a doubt that her heavenly Father knew and cared. Tasia drifted off into a deep sleep.

The ringing of the telephone jarred her awake. She opened her eyes to the room's familiar walls, the early morning light filtering through the window's lacy curtains. She glanced at the clock on the wooden nightstand next to her. *Eight o'clock.* Looking to her right, she realized Lizzie had left quietly without awakening her. She could hear voices in the distance.

Like it or not, the new day was upon her. With the Lord's help, she would get through this.

Wings clipped and warbling your anguished song –
Hopping on obstacles, not flying airborne;
Hiding in shadows, away from Love's throne –
Solitary soul, forlorn and feeling alone.

CS CHAPTER 28 ৪০

She decided on a simple closed casket ceremony. Better to remember him as vital and alive with a pictorial display of Ernie's life. Tasia's mother, brothers and family, dear friends and acquaintances, including Ernie's estranged brothers and sisters, came to pay their respects and lend supporting words of comfort the evening of his wake. Her friend Debbie also came to lend her emotional support. Tasia felt such peacefulness throughout the day, as though she were being held close to her Father's heart. Love was sustaining her.

The funeral was held the following cold, gray day. Everyone pitched in and took care of the details, relieving Tasia and her children to tend to more major concerns. Tasia's long-time friends from Mt. Prospect Bible Church days flew in from Vermont. Scott had since become a minister. Together he and his wife, Sue, pastored a church in Vermont. Scott spoke the eulogy. Pete, Josh and a mix of Tasia's and Ernie's brothers were pallbearers. She followed behind the casket until they laid it to rest over the frigid ground. A brief prayer was said and then the casket was lowered. The enormity of the moment weighed on Tasia as she fought to keep her emotions in check. She felt an arm slip around her shoulders and turned. Her dear mother. Did she know what she was feeling? Tasia patted her arm, thankfully.

How long she stood alongside the gaping pit, she couldn't say. At length, someone gently pulled her away. The emotional fog had returned. She was losing herself to a blurred, protective state of consciousness. Back at the house, family and friends had gathered and prepared a buffet for loved ones. By evening time, solitude once again settled upon the house.

A few evenings after the funeral, while Tasia was sorting through the necessary paperwork, Pete stopped by.

"Come on in, Pete. We're just sitting down in the kitchen. Want to join us?"

"Yeah, thanks." Pete walked past her, over to the table, and nodded at Josh and Lizzie. "There's something I want to get off my chest." He sat down and waited for Tasia to join them.

Tasia looked at his face. His brow was wrinkled and his mouth was drawn in tightly. His eyes narrowly squinted at her. "What is it, Pete?"

"Dad's whole death makes no sense to me. Dad's sister was right – it's *your* fault that he died!"

Tasia was speechless. Her mouth dropped open in disbelief.

Lizzie shot to her feet. "*What?* Pete, you don't know what you're saying."

Pete rose in return. "I know enough to know that Dad's death was needless." Pete turned toward Tasia. "*Mom*" – the word dripped with caustic sarcasm – "*how could you?*"

Josh pounded the table with his fist. "Enough of this. Pete, *you* weren't here when it happened. How *dare* you disrespect Mom like this!"

"Yeah, well, *neither* were you, Josh. How do you know what *really* happened?"

Lizzie walked right up to Pete, looking up at his beet-red face. "*I* was there, Pete. Do you want to accuse *me*, too? Besides, if there's going to be any accusing going on, I've got a few things to say about *you*." She turned and looked at Josh. "And I know Josh can back up every word."

Josh walked up to Pete and stood by his sister's side. "Okay, then, Pete. Mom still doesn't know anything about the bruises. So, let's get it out in the open right now."

Pete hesitated, then backed down. "That was a long time ago and *this* isn't the time or place to discuss it." He walked over to his coat, picked it up, and went to the door. "I'm *sick* of this family. If this is the way you treat family, I'm outta here." He stomped out the door, slamming it shut.

"That's fine by me," Josh said, making his way back to the table. Lizzie joined him. "Me, too."

Tasia turned her gaze from the door back to Josh and Lizzie. "Will one of you tell me what just happened?"

"It's nothing, Mom – just that when we were little, Pete used to hurt us."

Tasia's eyebrows furled together. "Hurt you? Hurt you how?" She looked at Lizzie, hoping to get some answers.

Lizzie volunteered. "I don't remember a whole lot, but I do remember waking up at night because of Pete. He made us promise not to tell you or dad."

"Not to tell us *what*?" Tasia turned back to Josh.

"Just mean, stupid stuff. Well, as soon as I got strong enough, Pete never messed with us again." Josh held up his arm in a flexing stance and breathed deeply like a big weight had just lifted off of him. "I never told you or Dad. You guys had enough stuff going on."

When Tasia returned to the classroom, her students greeted her with hugs and surprised her with a giant card they had made. Each one had signed their name in it. Some had drawn little pictures of hearts and flowers. Tasia wiped away her tears. Her heart was so full.

Teaching kept her involved and busy. Most days she did fine. She left early enough in the morning to prepare and set up before the bell rang and the children filtered into the classroom. She loved her third graders. Her students were a mix from all income levels, which sometimes created special learning challenges – from both sides of the spectrum. Some were classified as 'problem' students; others as 'advanced.' Economic backgrounds were unreliable indicators of character or potential, as Tasia watched even the most hardened respond to kindness with a desire to please – at least, they still did at this age.

As long as Tasia's mind was occupied with other matters, she handled the days better. Free time became her greatest obstacle. The inclination of her heart was to withdraw from others and wallow in her sorrow.

A couple of weeks went by before Tasia could even make it back to church. She arrived during the worship/song time and was able to slip in unnoticed. She *so needed* His comfort. As she opened her mouth to sing, the floodgates of tears opened, as waves of emotions washed over her. It was okay to cry.

At the strangest of times, a wave of sorrow would wash over Tasia. There was no predicting it. It could happen while grocery shopping or even just walking down the sidewalk. She found herself avoiding groups of people, not wanting to explain or apologize for her tears. Ernie was dead; she would never see him again, and she didn't know if he was with the Lord or not. Sometimes aloneness was less painful and awkward; nevertheless, she had to keep pushing forward.

Tasia hadn't noticed her new habit of walking with her head down, until one day on her way to class. The Lord, who had been so gentle with her, now admonished her, *Hold your head up—you're a daughter of the King.*

As Tasia lifted her head, that new awareness took hold of her heart. She *was* a daughter of the King - of the most high God! That reality hadn't changed in her life, despite the loss of her husband. God hadn't left her alone, although she still experienced moments of loneliness. Only the passage of time would change that. For now, this was a time of transition. She needed to find out who she was in her *own* right. She resolved to intentionally develop that identity. It felt good walking with her head upright again!

In His branches solid and firm
Your being will find rest –
In His embrace so reassuring
Is a haven to build your nest.

Cℬ CHAPTER 29 ℬ℧

That next year saw many changes. Grief is a strange emotion and it takes an investment of time for the soul to heal. But in Tasia's case, some decisions couldn't wait. There was only her income now for the three of them to live on.

Aware of the wisdom of not making major decisions too soon after the death of a spouse, yet feeling that familiar financial pinch, Tasia listened carefully as Lizzie and Josh encouraged her to look for more affordable housing. One of Tasia's sisters-in-law was a realtor and agreed to watch for potential properties.

The hunt led them further out to the boonies than they would have preferred, but prices were more affordable there. They finally found a place about twenty-five miles west of their Mt. Prospect home. With Lizzie graduating from high school near the end of May, it was an inopportune time to be changing schools. But unless she drove the distance every day, there was no choice. Being farther from their relatives and friends was also a compromise they would have to make.

The tri-level townhouse was part of a small association and, being only two years old, was still considered new construction. With a vaulted ceiling and skylights in the living room, Tasia was struck by the bright, airy feeling of the place. A stream wound its way through a farmer's field in the background, which she could see through the large sliding-glass doors that led to the wooden deck. The combined kitchen/dinette also conveyed that same open feeling with windows framing the outdoor spaciousness like an exquisite work of art. Josh could have his bedroom in the finished basement below. Lizzie and

Tasia could have the two top-floor bedrooms. They returned home to discuss it.

"It's nice, but Elgin's so far from everything," Josh complained.

"But the townhouse is near the expressway," countered Lizzie. "I'm going to have to do the drive, too, but I'd be willing to."

"I liked it, too," Tasia said. "It would be farther for me to get to work, too, so I know how you feel. But there are so many positives about the place. Let's take this to the Lord in prayer. Afterwards, we'll share our impressions of what He reveals to us."

Sitting around the kitchen table, the three joined hands, prayed aloud, and then just waited in the presence of the Lord. After a few moments of silence, they opened their eyes.

"Did God reveal anything to you?" Tasia asked, looking first at Josh and then at Lizzie.

The hues from the setting sun played against Lizzie's brown hair, showing red and golden highlights. Lizzie was first to speak. "I believe this is the place for us."

"Well, not me," Josh said, folding his hands stubbornly over his beefy chest.

Then Tasia said, "I saw a large hand moving over the Chicagoland area and then it stopped and rested over the area where the townhouse sits. The impression I got was that of all the places we could choose to live, He gives us this one."

Josh kept his arms folded and looked like a stiff cut-out. "I don't agree."

"Well, whatever we do, we all have to be in agreement, or we don't do it," Tasia said. "So, I guess we'll just keep looking."

The next day, her sister-in-law called. "Tasia, someone else has made an offer on that townhouse you looked at yesterday. If you're still interested in it, I need to submit an offer from you today."

Tasia hesitated, unconsciously rubbing her temple as she thought of Josh. "Let me give you a call back in a little bit, Sharon." Without even putting the phone down, she called Josh and explained the situation to him. "Josh, do you still feel the same way about that townhouse?"

"Mom, I told you last night how *I* felt about it. What I *didn't* tell you is what God had revealed to me when we were praying. That *is* the house He's led us to, Mom." He cleared his throat. "Sorry I didn't tell you sooner. Hope it's not too late for you to put a bid on it."

"That's okay, Josh. Thanks for your honesty, in spite of how I know you feel about it personally." Tasia took a deep breath. "Well, let's see what happens. Gotta go. I love you, Josh."

"Love you, too, Mom."

Tasia called Sharon back with a bid.

"No, it's not too late. How much? Okay, got it. I'll tell them your offer and get back to you as soon as I hear anything."

Okay, Lord, Tasia prayed silently. It's in Your hands now.

About an hour later, the phone rang again. "Hello, Tasia? When do you want to close?"

Tasia, Lizzie, Hershey, and a still-reluctant Josh moved into the townhouse in Elgin before the end of April. That last month of school was a long haul for Lizzie, who drove back and forth to classes each day. Finally, her high school graduation arrived. Tasia, wanting to make the occasion special for Lizzie, had saved up some money to celebrate over dinner at an upscale restaurant. The graduation ceremony went smoothly. Tasia tried to be upbeat for Lizzie, as she knew how hard this must be for her.

Afterwards, the three of them went to the restaurant and were soon shown to a round table with four chairs.

"We won't need that extra chair," Tasia told the maitre'd. Ernie's presence was sorely missed, yet no one brought him up in conversation. Finally, Tasia said, "Lizzie, we've all been through a lot, but I want you to know that Josh and I are so proud of you. I know you've worked so hard for this day, and if your Dad were here right now, he'd say the same thing. We've always been so proud of you." Tasia handed her daughter a small bouquet of flowers. Lizzie reached for them through her tears.

Life kept moving, relentlessly, ever forward. Lizzie was busy with preparations to leave for college in the fall. Most of Josh's time was spent working at First National Bank and visiting his friends back in the old neighborhood. They hadn't heard from Pete since the day he stormed out of their lives. There was no time for looking back. Her life was a whirlwind of constant flux.

Still batting the urge to withdraw from society, Tasia joined a block-party committee thinking it would be a good opportunity to meet some of her new neighbors.

After asking Tasia some questions about herself, Darlene, the committee chairperson and a vivacious social butterfly, said, "You know, there's a guy who lives around here who talks a lot like you do. Maybe he'll be at the block party and you'll have a chance to meet."

"Maybe," Tasia replied, half-heartedly. The last thing in the world she wanted right now was male involvement. One of the easiest ways to drive people away from her, especially guys, was by bringing 'God' into a conversation. Life was just too short to play games.

Tasia and her family were getting more acclimated to their new location with each passing month. As the mid-August date for the block party grew near, she actually began to look forward to meeting new people.

The afternoon of the party was sunny and hot. Tables were set up on the blacktop with a large barbecue grill toward the back. Everybody had been instructed to bring a side dish, so in addition to the supplied hot dogs and hamburgers, there was plenty of food to go around. Tasia made polite small talk with some of the people she met. Nice folks. She excused herself and walked toward the grill for a hamburger.

While she stood waiting, she noticed a guy who slightly resembled Sean Connery, with a more generous supply of scalp showing.

He approached her. "Hi, I'm Kurt." He held out his hand to shake hers.

"Nice to meet you, Kurt. I'm Tasia," she said, balancing her plate in one hand and extending the other in polite acknowledgement. He had a nice smile and seemed normal enough.

"So, what brought you here?" Kurt asked when she disclosed that she had just recently moved in.

He was easy to converse with and genuinely moved by the recent events in her life. Well, time to test the waters. Tasia mentioned how God had been so faithful to her.

"Are you a Christian?" Kurt asked between bites of his hotdog. He took a step toward the ice cooler, opened its lid, and selected a Coke.

"Yes, I am." There, Tasia thought, now you can turn tail and run.

"Me, too," Kurt said, his clear blue eyes brightening. He smiled a broad grin, showing his pearly white teeth. He popped the top and took a long sip. "Ah, that's so good."

"You must be the guy Darlene mentioned," Tasia said, as she explained the conversation she had with her friend earlier that month.

"That's funny, Darlene told *me* another Christian lady had moved into the neighborhood and might be here today," he said with a chuckle.

I'll always love you, be assured,
And am so thankful to have shared
In the journey of your lives so far –
While looking forward to what's ahead.

CƷ CHAPTER 30 ᏮᎧ

"Lizzie, come on – we're ready to go," shouted Tasia through the open driver's door of the rented van. She couldn't believe her little girl was all grown up and heading off to start college.

Lizzie was a full-grown young woman now who could turn the head of most young men. She wore her shoulder-length hair loosely gathered in a ponytail for this trip, with blue jeans and pink tank top. She seldom wore makeup – she didn't need to with her dark features and beautiful complexion.

Lizzie emerged from the garage carrying the last cardboard box to squeeze into the back. Josh pressed the remote control, the garage door lowered, and Tasia pressed the pedal. They were off to Winona.

Josh sat in the passenger seat next to Tasia. He pulled out the map and studied it. "About three hundred and fifty miles, as the crow flies. I figure we ought to be there before nightfall." Josh had become a handsome young man. He so resembled his father, both in looks and mannerisms. He was lean and muscular, standing at five feet, seven inches. His closely cropped hair was just a shade lighter than Ernie's had been. But it was his heart that was his best feature – he was a likeable person with a fair and considerate soul.

Lizzie was wedged in the back seat but still managed to buckle her seatbelt. "Can't believe it's really happening, Mom. I'm sure going to miss Hershey. Hope they take good care of him at the boarding place till you get back. Boy, everything's changing so fast!"

"I know what you mean, Lizzie." This was Tasia's first time out without wearing her gold wedding band. However, she wore its diamond accompaniment – her 'God is faithful' ring – on her right hand since its meaning extended far beyond that of a wedding ring.

As Josh had predicted, they made campus before nightfall. Josh did most of the carrying and moving of the boxes. When had he gotten so strong? Tasia and Lizzie carried whatever they could manage.

Soon Lizzie was all situated in her new dorm room. The time had come to say goodbye. "Thanks, Mom, for everything. Bro, you take good care of Mom, okay?"

"Okay, sis." They hugged one last time. "You be careful and do good, okay?" Josh's eyes started to get a little watery.

"I promise." Lizzie's eyes were brimming themselves. Lizzie reached out to hug Tasia one last time. "I'll miss you, Mom."

"I'll miss you, too, Lizzie." Tasia felt her eyes begin to water. Now was not the time, otherwise they'd all be crying. "I'll give you two rings when we get back home, just so you know we made it, okay? Goodbye, Lizzie – God bless you."

"God bless you, too. Goodbye…"

After refilling the tank, Tasia and Josh started the long trip back. This time, however, Josh drove. Along the way he disclosed something that had been on his mind for some time. "Mom, I'm not cut out for a behind-the-desk-type of job. The banking business is so dry. I need to do something I can do with my hands. I'm considering enrolling at a technical school to get certified in HVAC."

Tasia wasn't surprised. "Josh, part of finding a career path is knowing what you like to do. You're a very talented person in many ways, and you've always had a keen mind and natural curiosity. If you think this is the direction you want to follow, you've got my blessing. Go ahead and give it a try."

They pulled into the driveway just before midnight. Stepping out of the van, Tasia's legs felt rubbery against the solid pavement. "Whew, that was quite a trip! Thanks, Josh, I couldn't have done this without you. Whad'ya say we go give Lizzie her two rings and get to bed?"

Can you sit peacefully amidst the quiet?
Or walk joyfully through the rain?
Do you understand that misery grows
When you indulge your pain?

CB CHAPTER 31 BD

Friday night. Tasia was home – alone. The week at school had been busy and fulfilling. She was looking forward to some down time. She checked the messages on the answering machine. Lizzie had called, said she was doing fine and missed them. "Yeah, I miss you, too, Lizzie," Tasia mumbled. Josh was out for the evening. And Pete – well, he had walked out of her life once before and returned. Maybe it was a mixed blessing that he was gone. Maybe….

She was hungry and opened a can of tuna fish, eating it right from the can. What was the sense of making a meal – for just one? The house was so empty and quiet – too quiet. She walked over to the stereo in the living room and selected some praise tapes to play. That usually helped lift her spirits and get her mind off herself. Music filled the rooms, but wasn't permeating the void in her soul. Tasia knew she wasn't alone, but for some reason, tonight her head and heart weren't in synch. An indiscernible cloak of darkness hovered around her. She tried, but just couldn't shake off its heavy mantle.

Tasia sat on the stairs leading from the kitchen to the bedrooms, staring blankly at the darkness beyond the patio doors. Her chest heaved in anguish as loud sobs arose from her soul. Cupping her face in her hands, she cried in despair. "God – please help me!"

The loud, persistent ringing of the kitchen phone urged Tasia to answer. She got up slowly and walked zombie-like to the phone. "Hello?"

"Tasia, is that you? Are you all right?"

Tasia sobbed as she tried to speak. "Mom – I'm having such a hard time right now. I just can't seem to lift myself out of this – I miss Ernie so much…."

"Tasia, you know you're not alone. You've always had such a strong faith in God. Why, it's through you that I've come to know Him more fully. I'm sure He's with you even now. You know, Tasia, there's a difference between being lonely and being alone. You're going to have times when you're lonely. Everybody does. But Tasia, God will never leave you – you'll never be alone."

"I don't know, Mom – everything seems so dark – like there's a dark cloud over me that I can't shake. I'm so lonely, Mom!" Tasia's voice broke off between sobs. "Why did Ernie have to die just as we were dreaming and making plans for our future?" She paused again, this time coming back more firmly. "This is so hard!" Then, angrily. "It's just not fair!"

"Tasia, I surely don't have all the answers for you. But I do know that God is loving and good. The devil comes to steal, kill and destroy – not God. He takes care of His children. Tasia, He's taken care of you all along. He certainly isn't going to leave you now. You are loved, Tasia. Your father and I love you. Your children love you."

"I know, Mom, I really do. Please just talk to me awhile, okay? I can't think right now – think I'll just listen."

"Okay, Tasia. Would you like to hear about my day today?" She went on, rambling about the latest developments with the neighbors, Tasia's father, her brothers, and their children. "Are you still there, Tasia?"

She found the drone of her mother's voice soothing. "I'm still here, Mom – I'm doing better."

"Tasia, maybe sometimes we didn't always get along, but you are a dear daughter to me and I love you so much."

"Oh, Mom, I know – and I'm glad God made me your daughter, too." She hesitated and rubbed her temples before continuing. "Did you know your call just now was an answer to prayer?"

"How so, Tasia?"

"I cried out for help and you called. You helped restore my focus, Mom – you helped lift me back up."

"I did?"

"Yeah – and I think I'm okay again. Thanks, Mom." Tasia rose to her feet. "Oh, and Mom?"

"Yes?"

"I love you."

"I love you, too, Tasia. I always have and I always will."

"I know, Mom. Thanks."

Tasia hung the phone back in its cradle, put on another tape and grabbed her Bible. As she sat at the kitchen table, she flipped through the pages until it opened at Psalm 63. Her eyes fell on the word 'bed'. She turned and gazed at the darkness framed through the windows. Her bed was such an empty place – another night to get through. The words *lonely, but not alone* rang in her consciousness. Yes, she needed to hold onto that reality. Glancing back to the page, she read: "On my bed I remember you; I think of you through the watches of the night." Yes, God, I do. "Because you are my help, I sing in the shadow of your wings." God, that's where I want to be. "My soul clings to you; your right hand upholds me." God, that's what I need.

Cognition was becoming reality. She was not alone. Things would be all right. Slowly, tenderly, the tear in her heart was beginning to mend. The seeds of her new identity were being planted.

The morning sun streamed through the bedroom window, inviting Tasia to join the new day. Hershey nudged her with his cold, wet nose, waiting impatiently for her to get dressed and take him out for his morning walk. Along the way, she encountered a familiar face.

Kurt turned toward her and smiled. "Well, up bright and early, I see. Wonder if there's any good news in the mail for me today?"

Tasia smiled back. "Yep, some things just can't be put off." Hershey tugged on the leash, straining to explore the scents further ahead. "Well, looks like I'll have to catch you later." Tasia started to walk away, with Hershey in the lead.

"Will you be home this morning? Maybe we could talk more over a cup of cappuccino."

Tasia called over her shoulder. "Sure, but all I've got is regular coffee."

"No problem. See you in a bit."

Kurt showed up about an hour later carrying a cappuccino maker. "Can't beat that. Not only do I invite myself over, but I bring my own coffee machine with me!" He laughed freely – easily, as he held out the maker.

She smiled widely. "Cool – cappuccino's my favorite." Tasia invited him in and led the way upstairs to the kitchen, where Kurt showed her how to operate the machine. They sat outside on the wooden deck overlooking the sleepily rolling creek. A small herd of deer were visible at the far end of the cornfield, near the tree line. Kurt was a regional maintenance administrator for a national property management company and was temporarily home between assignments.

"There's something I need to let you know straight off, Tasia. I got divorced last year. It was pretty painful." He settled back in the plastic lawn chair. "I know when I met you, you mentioned that you've recently been widowed. I just don't want there to be any crossed signals. I'm not looking for any relationships or entanglements. Besides, I'm obviously older than you are."

Tasia edged forward in her seat. "Well, that's good 'cause believe me, neither am I," she said. "I hope we can just be friends, no matter what our ages might be. By the way, as long as you brought it up, how old are you?" She looked at him, smiling, like one who's just laid the gauntlet down.

He wasn't quite ready to pick it up. "Don't let the gray hair fool you. I started turning gray in my thirties. Take a guess – how old do you think I am?" He returned her grin, his moustache hiding his upper lip.

Tasia studied his face. "Hmm, gray hair and laugh crinkles aside, I'm thinkin' fiftyish."

Kurt chuckled softly. "Not a bad guess, at that. Tack on an extra three years and you've got it." He looked at her with his kind blue eyes, his voice teasing. "Okay, my turn. After all, turn about, as they say, is fair play."

"Okay," Tasia said coyly. "Let's see how close you come."

Now it was his turn to study her face. "Hmm, I'm thinkin'... I'm

thinkin' you're way too young for me! But however old you are,
God's done a good job!"

They both laughed.

Tasia reached for her cup and sat back in her chair. "Okay, I'll
'fess up. Try forty-two on for size."

"You wouldn't lie to a friend, would you?" Kurt's eyes were
shining playfully at her.

"Well, that's the beauty of friendship – age doesn't matter, right?"
She smiled more to herself than to Kurt. She was enjoying this bantering
exchange. "I didn't realize how much I missed talking to a man, let
alone one who likes talking about 'God' stuff, too."

Kurt reached for his cup and took a sip. "Yeah, I know what you
mean. Sometimes it's nice just to have a friend to talk to. I know
when I've been out for months on different assignments around the
country, sometimes I get so lonely, missing someone to talk to or do
stuff with. I used to frequent book stores a lot, as well as movie
theaters and restaurants. I love my job, but as interesting as all of that
is, it's always good to come back home to family."

'Family' turned out to be his mother, brothers and their families,
and his two grown sons, one of whom lived out-of-state and had a
family of his own. The second of four sons, Kurt's father had died
when he was a six-year-old child. His mother wasn't able to care for
them all, so he and his older brother had spent most of his childhood
in a school for fatherless boys. "I did spend a few years with my
grandparents in Bakersfield, California, though. Those were special
years for me," Kurt recalled.

"Bakersfield – the 'armpit' of the world?" Tasia giggled.

Kurt's bushy white eyebrows knit together. "Armpit? That's the
first time I've ever heard it called that."

"We lived in Sacramento for a couple of years and drove through
Bakersfield once or twice. Trust me – it's aptly named. I've never
experienced driving through a town that smelled so rancid and *putrid*!"
Tasia stressed the last few words even more loudly than she'd intended,
over the whirring of a nearby lawnmower.

"Well, when I was there, the air was fresh and clean. You could
see the surrounding mountains outlining the town like a protective

barrier." Kurt breathed in the fresh, sweet smell of freshly cut grass that wafted upward in the breeze.

"And years later, when we traveled through it, that mountainous barrier could barely be seen through all the pollution." Tasia wrinkled up her nose in remembrance.

They continued chatting until she looked at her watch. "Kurt, it's really been nice getting to know you, but I've got to get on with my day."

"Yeah, me, too." He slid open the patio door. "Ladies first," he said.

Tasia chuckled. "Well, thank you, sir." She led him to the kitchen so he could take his cappuccino maker back home with him.

"Tell you what, Tasia. Since you enjoy it so much, I'll let you borrow it. Feel free to use it, but on one condition."

"Uh, oh – that depends. What condition?"

"That we can get together again for another cup of cappuccino some time."

"Perhaps that can be arranged," said Tasia airily and then laughed comfortably.

He joined in. "Good, then I'll be off." He sauntered to the front door. "See you later, friend."

"See ya." She closed the door. Hmm, how 'bout that!

How interesting, this round thing I found –
Half exposed and half of it hidden,
I clasped my hands around its form
Seeking to free it from its prison.

CB CHAPTER 32 BO

Over the course of the next few months, Tasia and Kurt met together for coffee and conversation a few more times. Tasia enjoyed his company. He had such an easy way of making her laugh. The doorbell rang. Hershey beat her to it.

Grabbing Hershey by his collar, she scolded, "Down, Hershey." "Hi, Kurt. Come on in."

Tasia prepared the cappuccino as Kurt went to the table. Hershey lay at his feet as he petted him. "Tasia, I'm being transferred to another location and may be gone a couple of years. We've become good friends and I don't want to leave you with any false expectations."

"What do you mean, 'false expectations'?" She brought their cups to the table and set them down.

"You've become a good friend, Tasia, but sometimes good friendships go further. I want you to know that was never my intention with you. I just don't have room for any other involvements right now." His normally twinkling eyes changed to watery blue depths, his lips relaxed, but closed in a straight line.

Tasia sat down and studied his face, her eyes narrowing a bit, her right eyebrow slightly upraised. "By 'involvements' do you mean we won't be friends anymore – or are you talking about this going to a deeper level?"

"I mean a deeper level, Tasia. I'd like to just stay your friend." His face brightened a bit as he continued, "I'll be back periodically from my assignment to see my family, though. Maybe when I'm back, I could call you and we could talk."

This was really strange. Why was he saying any of this at all? "Kurt, let me be perfectly honest with you. I enjoy talking with you and do consider you a friend also. I'm sorry to hear you're leaving, but if you'd like to give me a call when you're in town, that's fine with me." She turned and glanced downward, feeling a check in her spirit. What there something more? Raising her eyes to his, she lifted her hands. Turning them palm-side up, she openly cupped them loosely together as if a delicate butterfly had alighted and she was holding it up to a passing breeze to continue its flight. "Kurt, you are my friend. I will hold onto you this tight."

His eyes twinkled and his smile returned. "Tasia, that's the most freeing thing I've ever heard."

As their conversation wound down, Tasia rose to walk Kurt to the door. Passing through the kitchen, she halted. "Oh, do you want to wait a minute while I clean your cappuccino maker? It'll just take a second."

"Nah. You might as well just keep it here and use it till next time." He continued his way to the stairs and down to the front door. "Well, Tasia, you take care."

Tasia caught up to him. They hugged briefly, as friends might. She patted him on his back. "You, too, Kurt. Have a safe trip."

He turned and waved goodbye before heading down the block.

Tasia glanced at her watch. *One-thirty?* Time to get the old proverbial show on the road. There were things to do, places to go, people to see before her dance class that evening at seven – one of many new adventures she was exploring. *Swing* was the popular dance of the day. She was going to get out and give it a whirl.

Alas – to free it proved beyond
This mortal one's endeavors.
One year passed, and then another
Before any more encounters.

CHAPTER 33 ☙

A few years had passed since Ernie's death. Tasia was forging ahead, undergoing her own metamorphosis. Little by little, one step at a time, God was molding and reshaping her, healing and redefining her, strengthening and preparing her.

She found great fulfillment in teaching, although each year became more challenging. Tasia got a job in the Elgin school district teaching third grade. Even more so than her previous classes in Mt. Prospect, these students came from quite a jumbled mix of economic backgrounds and experiences. Her third graders were caught somewhere between childhood naïveté and preteen precociousness. Some were too street savvy and experienced for their young years, while others were still somewhat sheltered and innocent.

Tasia was beginning to enjoy her freedom as a single woman. Finances were still tight, but she and the kids were getting by on her teacher's salary. Josh encouraged his mom to go out more often and have fun. She did enjoy getting out and socializing with her girlfriends. She also began to date. At first it felt strange, but she found she enjoyed the companionship of other men. Each time a man came to pick her up, Josh made sure he was on hand to meet him. Yet, each time, his on-the-side comments to her were disparaging. "Mom, he looks like a loser"; or "Mom, I don't like the looks of him"; or "He's not your type, Mom." Tasia would just smile and give him a hug and kiss – she knew it was difficult for her son to see her go out with any man other than his father.

Dating hadn't changed all that much over the years. She was careful to date only guys that she knew were Christians. Although she missed love's touch, she didn't want to risk getting involved with anyone who didn't share her beliefs or sexual boundaries. If ever there were to be another man in her life, he would have to be one God had chosen for her, one who loved the Lord with all his heart. That way, she reasoned, everything else in his life would also be in orderly balance.

Tasia was surprised that she hadn't heard another word from Kurt after their last coffee together. She had called his house a couple of times and left messages for him to pick up his coffee maker, but he hadn't returned them.

She tried one last time. "Hello, Kurt, this is Tasia down the street. I've left you a couple of voicemail messages over the last year or so, but you've never called back. Frankly, at this point, I have no idea whether you're alive or dead, but if you still want your cappuccino machine, I have it." She hung up the phone and shook her head – it just didn't make any sense. She had thought they were friends. Well, she was getting used to things not making sense in this world.

Thank You, Father, for Your love –
You are the Faithful One and True.
You fill my heart with satisfaction –
Every day is new.

Cß CHAPTER 34 ßつ

The shrill sound of the alarm clock awoke Tasia with a jolt. Instinctively, her hand jerked up and pressed the button, filling the room with silence. She lay in the stillness of the moment, collecting her thoughts. *Sunday morning.*

The alarm woke Hershey up, too. He bounded into her bedroom and sat obediently at her bedside, his thick tail beating anxiously against the bed frame. "Good morning, Hershey. I'll be with you in a few minutes. " She rolled over to the side of the bed and soon felt a cold nose against her arm. She laughed. "Okay, Hershey, but you gotta give me a break!"

Getting out of bed, Tasia slid her feet into terry-cloth slippers and quietly tiptoed toward the kitchen. Soon the popping of the percolator broke the stillness of the hour, releasing the aroma of its fresh French-roasted brew. She poured herself a cup of coffee and sat down at the table, gazing blankly at the panoramic view through the kitchen window. Hershey lay at her feet, his tail thumping impatiently on the floor.

"Yes, Hershey, I get the point." Tasia donned her coat, hooked Hershey's leash and flew out the door to a nearby tree. Relieved, he quickly ran back to the door. Tasia chuckled, "Don't want to stay out in the cold any longer than you have to, eh?"

Back inside, Tasia looked at the clock on the living room wall. Eight o'clock. She would have just enough time to get ready, grab a quick bowl of cereal, and make it in time for Sunday School. She reflected for a moment back to when Pete, Josh, and Lizzie were younger and they had accompanied Tasia to another church, attending as a family. But they were all adults now, each responsible for their own relationship with the Lord. Tasia missed that sense of togetherness.

Well, there was no use dwelling on the past.

Presently, she taught Sunday School to the third- through fifth-graders at a local church. Elgin Vineyard was comprised of a variety of people from many walks of life, a small composite representative of the area in general. Since the moment she first stepped through its doors, she was welcomed like family. Tasia enjoyed the worshipful mix between singing the reverent hymns and more upbeat songs, as well as listening to the pastor's style of teaching.

After his message on the value of the family unit, the pastor extended an invitation to heads of households to come forward to receive special prayer. Several men and women, as well as Tasia, walked to the front of the sanctuary. Others were invited to come and pray for them. As Tasia stood, she felt a hand lay on her shoulder as a lady's voice prayed. When she was done, she removed her hand from Tasia. Tasia turned and recognized Chris, a friend from church with the gift of prophecy. "Thanks for praying for me, Chris."

The petite older lady replied, "God has a message for you, Tasia." Her face was so serene – her dark eyes resembled peaceful pools of water.

Tasia's hazel eyes widened in contrast. "Okay, Chris, go ahead. I'm all ears."

"God says He has a Christian husband for you."

Tasia rubbed the side of her head. Well, it couldn't be the guy she broke up with just the other week. And she wasn't seeing anyone currently. "Thanks for the message, but only God knows who it could be."

Two weeks later, Tasia was back in church singing with the rest of the congregation. Unexpectedly, the message, *'I'm going to do something new in your life'* shot across Tasia's mind.

"Is that You, Lord?"

The message repeated itself.

"Lord, what do You mean?"

Silence.

"Okay, Lord – whatever it is, I know You'll see me through it."

The week flew by. Lizzie would be arriving home Saturday for Christmas break. There was a lot to do beforehand.

On Friday, a large winter storm hit the Midwest. Tasia was concerned for Lizzie's safety, knowing first-hand how treacherous the roads could be. As much as she looked forward to seeing her daughter again, she would have preferred that Lizzie not risk the drive, especially with her aging car and balding tires. But Lizzie was determined. Thankfully, after driving all night through the blinding snow, she arrived safe, sound, and exhausted. Her family was momentarily under one roof again – well, almost the entire family.

You alighted into my life –
This bird set free to soar,
Enabled to sing life's melody –
Released to love once more.

CS CHAPTER 35 &O

Christmas was not one of Tasia's favorite holidays. Oh, the meaning behind it was great, but it was always a reminder of that *other* day. Perhaps that's why it had been so important for Lizzie to be with her family. Hoping to add something uplifting to the holiday season, Tasia purchased tickets to attend Moody Bible Institute's Christmas caroling chorale. Josh had made other plans, so it was girls' night out. The inspiring event was well worth the drive and the cost. On the way home, they stopped for some hot chocolate and a chance to catch up. Tasia pulled into the Rock N Roll McDonald's. The place was hopping. Lizzie spied a little corner booth and quickly grabbed it, while Tasia went and ordered.

After Tasia was seated, Lizzie gently blew across the top of her paper cup and took a test sip. "Hmm, pretty hot stuff. Thanks, Mom, this is really nice."

Tasia's eyes glistened. "Oh, Lizzie, you have no idea how special this has been for me, too. It's such a delight to be with you again." Tasia sampled a sip as well. "Boy, that is good. So, Lizzie, how's school going?"

"Well, that's actually one of the things I wanted to discuss with you, Mom." Lizzie edged forward in her seat. "I've changed my major from teaching to social work. I believe that'll be a more open-ended career choice for me. What do you think?"

Tasia looked in her daughter's bright hazel eyes. They were full of hope and expectancy. "Honestly, Lizzie, I'm not surprised. I always knew God gave you a tender heart for people. You certainly have the sensitivity and level-headedness for it." Tasia broke into a smile, "Never could picture you or Josh stuck inside some stuffy ol' office building day in and day out at a nine-to-five desk job."

They laughed and continued chatting a while longer. Soon they were back on the expressway headed for home.

As Tasia pulled into their subdivision, she noticed another car following closely behind her. It tailgated her right to her driveway. "Hmm…Lizzie, there's a familiar-looking car behind us, but I can't make out who it is." Lizzie turned to look, as Tasia got out and saw a figure emerge from behind the steering wheel. "Well, what d'ya know."

"Hi, Tasia – it's been awhile! I thought that was you ahead of me."

Lizzie was out of the car now, too. "Oh, hi, Kurt. How ya doing?"

"Great, Lizzie. Home for Christmas break, I see."

"Yeah, and we just got home from a concert in the city." Lizzie's body shivered beneath her woolen coat. "Want to come in? It's cold out here."

Tasia shivered, too, but wasn't so sure she wanted Kurt in her house. "I'll join you soon, Lizzie." Turning her attention back to Kurt, she said, "I'm surprised to see you again, Kurt. I didn't know if you were still alive on planet earth."

The twinkle in Kurt's eyes dimmed slightly. "Oh, that. Sorry, Tasia. I've never been much of a phone person. Got your messages, though. A couple of times when I was in town, I even saw you walking Hershey in the early morning, so I knew you were still around."

Why should it have mattered to her anyway? "Well, friends or not, what brings you around?" The sharp words hit their mark.

Kurt stepped back slightly, grabbing his chest. "Ouch, that hurt! Guess I deserved that. Tasia, I do value our friendship. Maybe it won't make much sense to you right now, but I'm gun shy when it comes to relationships. I've had too many failures." Then the familiar twinkle returned to his eyes. His words spilled out quickly with excitement. "Anyway, the most amazing thing happened tonight. I was driving from an assignment in Ohio to a new one in St. Louis, when I got a call asking if I would assume management of one of the company's properties here in the Chicagoland area. Of course, I said 'Yes.'" He paused and took a breath. "I have no idea why God's got me here, but here I am." Kurt held his arms out open wide.

Tasia smiled. There was definitely something different about this particular guy. "Well, if God brought you here, I'm sure he's not going to keep you on a shelf." Tasia started heading toward the door.

"Yeah, guess not. Hey, you still have that cappuccino maker, don't you?" Before she could answer, he continued, "Want to get together for coffee again? How 'bout tomorrow afternoon?"

Tasia's toes were starting to feel numb. She needed to get inside. "That might be a problem. A piece broke off, so it's not working right."

"Well then, all the more reason. I just happen to be mechanically inclined, you know." He chuckled as he opened his car door. "See you tomorrow?"

"All right," Tasia nodded and watched him pull away, closing the door behind her. Man, it was cold outside.

The cappuccino maker needed a new part. Although Tasia had coffee on hand, Kurt offered to take her to Boston Chicken. "It's not like this is a date or anything like that, Tasia. I'm just plain hungry."

The holidays went as quickly as they came. With everybody's busy schedules, holidays were one of the few times they all got together. This year they all met at her brother Ken's house on Christmas Day. Between all her nieces and nephews, family get-togethers had become quite an affair. To make it easier on everyone, they rotated holidays at each other's homes.

After New Year's Day, Lizzie had to head back to school. Closing the car door after loading her now-clean laundry, she was ready to hit the road. She gave her mom a big hug. "Thanks again for everything, Mom. It was a good break...I sure needed it!"

Josh was next to give her a hug. "I'll miss you, little sis. You drive safe and keep your nose to the grindstone."

"Yeah, will do. I'll miss you, too, big bro. Hey, you take care of things while I'm away, okay?"

Josh nodded.

Lizzie headed down the driveway, but not before Tasia could get her last words in. "God bless you, Lizzie. I love you. Give us two rings when you get there."

"Okay, Mom." And she was off.

The following week Kurt called and asked Tasia if she'd like to go see a show with him on Saturday night. Titanic was playing and Kurt wanted to see it on the wide screen. Tasia wanted to see it, too.

As the time approached for Kurt to pick her up, Tasia thought she would let Josh know her plans. "Josh, Kurt should be over shortly. We're going to see Titanic tonight. What about you? Got any plans?"

"Yeah, going to get together with a couple of the guys. Maybe have a jam session." Josh paused and then continued, "Mom, Kurt's been around more lately than he ever was. What's up with that?"

"I guess because he's been gone awhile, he's just happy to have the company."

"You sure that's all?"

"As far as I know, Josh. Why? What do you think of him?"

"Oh, I guess he's all right. Talks a little too much for my liking, though."

"Then I guess it's a good thing that you're not the one going to the show with him tonight." Tasia chuckled and smiled at Josh. "Don't worry, Josh, there's nothing serious going on between Kurt and me."

Just then the doorbell rang. Tasia answered it and invited Kurt inside while she got her coat out of the closet.

He noticed Josh standing at the top of the stairway. "Hey, Josh, how's it going?"

"Good as it can be. How 'bout you, Kurt?"

"Just fine, man." He reached for Tasia's coat, holding it for her as she slipped into it.

Tasia turned and faced him point blank. "So, Kurt, I just want to set the record straight. We're going out to see a show together tonight, but it's not a date, right?"

Kurt reached up and fingered his moustache. "Glad you brought that up, Tasia. Somebody told me they thought you might be kind of sweet on me. Is that true?"

Talk about turning the tables! Truth was, though, she did think he was sort of nice. Well, two could play at this game. Trying to keep a straight face, she asked, "What in the world would make you think such a thing?"

Kurt's blue eyes dimmed, but he never took them off of her. "Oh, I dunno – maybe they were mistaken."

Tasia didn't have the heart to keep up the charade. "Well, you certainly don't repulse me – truth is, I do find you rather attractive."

The light returned to his baby blues. "Oh – good – I mean, I was just wonderin'. Well then, whad'ya say we get this show on the road?" Glancing upward, he said, "Goodbye, Josh."

Tasia finished buttoning her coat and grabbed her purse. "See you later, Josh. Be safe." If Tasia had looked more closely, she would have noticed that her son was only half smiling.

"Yeah, you too, Mom. Goodnight."

Spiritual expressions
Experienced in tangible ways –
God's love cascades upon me
In series of billowing waves.

☙ CHAPTER 36 ❧

Hershey's normally voracious appetite slowed, and every now and then Tasia noticed red spots on the light-colored carpeting. "Josh, I'm concerned about Hershey. Want to come to the vet with me Saturday?"

"I can't, Mom – work's got me scheduled through the weekend. Not that I'm complaining. I can sure use the extra money." Josh called Hershey over to where he sat on the couch and looked into his chocolate-brown eyes. "Yeah, he doesn't look right to me, either. Even his eyes aren't as bright as they normally are."

Tasia and Hershey were among the first ones at the animal hospital that morning. After a thorough examination, the vet said, "Mrs. Franklin, it looks like a prostate problem. I can give you something to help ease his discomfort, but even with an operation, there's no guarantee. The choice is up to you."

Tasia stroked Hershey's head. "Well, doc, I haven't got much money, but I don't want Hershey to suffer, either."

"If he were my dog, I'd make it as easy as possible for him. I'll have my assistant give you some pills for Hershey. Just give him one, preferably with food, in the morning. If the bleeding continues, give me a call."

"All right, doc. Thanks." Tasia hooked Hershey's leash to his collar and walked back to the desk next to the waiting room. By now, the room was full of animals meowing and barking, being restrained by their owners. Hershey normally would have tugged on the leash to go join in the action, but today he just stayed at Tasia's side while she paid the bill.

"Come on, Hershey, let's go home."

The spotting stopped, but over the next few weeks, Hershey's appetite continued to wane. Moving became more and more of an effort. One day when Tasia came home from school, Hershey didn't greet her at the front door. "Hello, Hershey, I'm home," Tasia called, waiting for the sound of his bounding body to come meet her. But not this day. She took off her coat and changed her shoes. "Hershey, where are you?" She climbed up the stairs and saw Hershey laying under the coffee table in the living room.

Tasia bent down to check on him. "Hershey?" His legs were stiff, but his body was still warm to the touch. "Oh, Hershey…." Tears welled up in her eyes and spilled over. She slowly walked over to the phone and called Kurt.

"The party you have called is unavailable. Please leave your name and number at the sound of the tone."

Through her sobbing, she managed to leave Kurt a message about what happened. "…And don't worry about me, Kurt. I'll try calling Josh. Goodbye."

She dialed Josh and left him a voicemail message, too. A few minutes later, the phone rang. "Hi, Mom? Got your message. I'm on my way home."

"But, Josh, what about your job?"

"I called my boss and explained the situation. He's sending someone else to cover for me. I should be there in thirty minutes." Click.

Josh arrived and together they worked a sheet under Hershey's body and carried him to the car. Tasia had already called the animal hospital's emergency line. They were waiting, prepared to take care of his body upon their arrival.

The car ride home was quiet. When they entered the house, Josh turned on the television. "It's just too quiet in here."

Tasia busied herself washing the rug where Hershey's body had lain.

Just then, the doorbell rang. Josh went to see who it was. "Mom, it's Kurt," he called out, unenthusiastically.

"Let him in, Josh. He's probably responding to my earlier call tonight."

Josh opened the door. "Hi, Kurt. C'mon in."

"Thanks, Josh – got your mother's message about Hershey." Kurt looked over Josh's shoulder as Tasia was coming down the stairs.

"Hi, Kurt." Tasia walked over to him while Josh stepped away. Kurt gave Tasia a hug. "Got your message, Tasia. I'm so sorry I wasn't here for you. When I got your message, it just about broke my heart. You sounded so sad…I'm sorry about Hershey." Looking around for Josh, he continued, "But I see Josh has already taken care of things."

"Yeah, he called back right away. Thanks for comin' by to check on me, Kurt, but I'm all right, now." Tasia gave him a hug back and walked him toward the door.

"Okay, Tasia. I'll talk to you soon…goodnight."

"Good night, Kurt."

Gradually Tasia and Josh got used to Hershey's absence – another transition. And then yet another – Kurt started inviting Tasia to dinner on a regular basis. Their friendship was strengthening.

Springtime washed away the last traces of winter. As the budding leaves began opening to the sun's warmth, their friendship began deepening into a dating relationship. They spent the summer months together doing out-of-doors activities like going on bike hikes and picnics. Tasia felt happy when she was with him.

One Saturday afternoon along the bike path, Kurt's bike chain came off and he took a spill.

Tasia stopped and came over to his side. "You okay, Kurt?"

He chuckled and gave her a hug. "Tasia, I think I'm falling for you!" He looked into her eyes, "Tasia, may I kiss you?"

She smiled, "Right here…right now?" She felt his hands gently caress her face as he brought his closer, then the gentle touch of his lips on hers – so sweet and light – then gone. Shivers shot through her. She opened her eyes and saw his lips smiling back at her.

"I've been wanting to do that for the longest time," Kurt said, "but sure didn't expect that reaction."

They laughed. Kurt got his bike chain on and soon they were riding back along the path, heading toward home.

"Good night, Tasia. Pick you up for lunch tomorrow after church?"

"Yeah, that'd be nice, Kurt. See you later. Thanks for a nice afternoon."

"Boy, wasn't it a great day?" He sniffed the air and cupped a hand over his ear. "I think I hear a shower callin' my name." He leaned toward her and took her hand, resting it in the palm of his. Looking up at her, he smiled, "See you tomorrow, beauty." He pivoted and got back on his bike, waving goodbye.

Yeah, this guy was definitely something else!

I am that rose
Enriched by sorrow –
Opened to the Son's light
For a fragrant tomorrow!

☙ CHAPTER 37 ❧

"Kurt, there's something I need to tell you," Tasia said as they left church, walking hand-in-hand toward his car.

"Sure, Tasia – I'm all ears." He slowed his pace in keeping with hers, till they were completely standing still.

Tasia let go of his hand. "Kurt, there's something you should know about me before this goes any further." She looked at his furled brow. "You believe in the gift of prophecy, right?"

Kurt nodded, his eyes never leaving her.

Tasia bit down on her lower lip slightly. "Well, a friend of mine prayed with me once and told me that the Lord had a Christian husband for me." She looked up at his eyes. They were following her every move. Tasia lowered her eyes. "Not long after that, maybe a couple of weeks later, the Lord spoke to me and said He was going to do something new in my life." She paused and looked back up at Kurt, hoping to catch some sort of reaction.

His face looked blank.

She forged ahead, looking straight into his eyes. "So…if you want to run away from me now, I wouldn't blame you a bit."

Slowly, she saw Kurt's lips begin to curl upward, his eyes brightening. "So that's supposed to scare me off?"

That sure wasn't the reaction Tasia had expected. She wasn't sure what to say in response.

He noticed her eyebrow rise slightly as she gently rubbed her temple with her fingers. He reached for her hands and held them tenderly. "Now more than anything, it only confirms for me what I've been feeling for a long time now. Tasia, I love you. I believe that God has brought us together – that this is no coincidence. I believe *I* am that man."

"Oh, Kurt…I'm just not sure that *I'm* ready. There's so much to consider first." Tasia's pulse began to quicken.

"Then we'll leave it in the Lord's hands. He'll let us know." He patted her hands and released them, gently kissing her.

"Thanks, Kurt, that is the best way," Tasia agreed. "I've got to hear from Him first."

Summer gave way to autumn. Tasia had her new class of third-graders. Lizzie returned to Winona State University to complete her senior year. Josh had his own apartment. The only thing still unresolved was Tasia's relationship with Kurt. During the preceding weeks, Tasia had had opportunities to consult with her mom, Josh and Lizzie, and several of her friends.

Autumn usually brought a tinge of sadness to Tasia, as nature gave one final gasp of glory before being blanketed in snowy sleep. This afternoon, she felt drawn to drive to a nearby forest preserve and walk once more along its paths. This place was special to her. When Tasia had first moved to Elgin and discovered this preserve, she often drove to it after school with Hershey in tow. They would walk along its meadows of tall grass and wild flowers, and climb its tree-studded hills. The same creek that ran behind her townhouse snaked its way through this preserve on its way to join the Fox River. Hershey had loved to play in its icy water and roll in the sweet-smelling grass. It seemed the only constant in life was change.

Tasia listened to the tree branches bending against the gusty currents of wind. The brisk air was pungent with the acrid smell of decaying acorns and decomposing leaves, having long since seen their glory days. Even the leaves crunching beneath her feet as she walked would eventually dissolve to dust. The stately trees stood tall as a testimony, having withstood so many seasonal changes and weathered countless storms, driving their roots ever deeper into their supporting foundation.

Tasia walked over to her favorite tree – a vast, sprawling oak standing alone in the center of a meadow. Tasia, too, had come through many seasons of life and withstood its storms. She had sunk her roots deeper into her Foundation and emerged a testimony of her Creator's faithfulness. Little did she know, however, that her glory days were just beginning.

"*You will be his wife.*"

Tasia knew that voice. "Really, Lord?"

"*You will be his wife.*"

Her heart quickened; her mind began to race. Suddenly, all indecision vanished. All the pieces fit. "Thank you, Lord!" she called out to the expansive sky above her and headed toward her car.

She arrived home to a message from Kurt on her answering machine. "Tasia, I'll be over a little earlier tonight. Can you be ready by 4 o'clock? Unless I hear otherwise, I'll just plan on coming over. I've got some interesting news. Bye."

Tasia smiled. *And he thinks he's got interesting news.*

Kurt came over as planned, almost to the minute. "Hi, Tasia. Ready, m'lady?"

She already had her coat on and just reached for her purse. "Ready, teddy."

He walked with her to her car door and opened it. Before she sat down, she kissed him lightly. "Thanks, Kurt."

He winked and soon they were off. "Any place in particular you'd like to go for dinner tonight, Tasia?" He glanced at her and did a double-take. Her eyes were shining like emeralds. She was positively glowing.

Tasia couldn't wait to tell Kurt the news, but not just yet. "It doesn't really matter to me, Kurt. Do you have something special in mind?"

"Actually, I do. Let's go to Macaroni's then, all right?"

"Sounds good to me," Tasia said, turning up the heat a little.

There was plenty of parking when they arrived and they were able to get choice seating. Their waitress came and introduced herself by writing her name on the paper tablecloth. "Hi, folks. As you can see, my name's Sandy and I'll be your server this evening. Would you like to start with an appetizer before dinner?"

Kurt ordered a sampler. As they waited for their food, Kurt shared his news with Tasia. "Tasia, I finally got together with Josh today. We met for lunch and had a good conversation. Among the topics we discussed was the possibility of you and I getting married. You should be proud, Tasia – you and Ernie raised quite a fine young man. He feels very protective toward you and loves you very much. We had a very frank discussion."

Kurt definitely had piqued her attention. Her eyes widened as she leaned forward on the table's edge. "What'd he say about 'us'?"

Kurt smiled as he recounted their conversation. "He said it's been hard for him to see you with me, especially since he loved his dad so much and I'm so different from Ernie. I told him that I would never try to replace his dad, but hopefully could be a good friend to both him and his sister." Kurt paused to catch his train of thought. "He said he gave his permission for me to ask for your hand in marriage – said he'd be proud to have me as a stepdad. Then he thanked me for talking with him – that it meant a lot. Before we left, I went to shake his hand and we hugged. He even got a bit teary-eyed. And to tell you the truth, Tasia, so did I."

Tasia took a deep breath. That was big news, indeed. "Oh, Kurt, I'm so happy to hear that!"

"That's not all. Josh gave me Lizzie's phone number at school. I tried calling her when I got back home and caught her just as she was on her way out. I quickly explained that I had just met with Josh and also wanted her permission to ask you to marry me." His eyes were twinkling.

"And?" Like she didn't already know.

"And she said of course it was. We just talked briefly, but she sends you her love."

Tasia smiled. That sounded like her Lizzie.

Kurt reached into his coat pocket and handed his date a card.

She opened it and smiled, as she read its contents asking if she wanted to be his friend. Did she want to be his friend? Boy, if he only knew. "Yes, Kurt, I love being your friend."

Kurt looked pleased with her answer. "Good – me, too." He reached back into his pocket and produced a second card, which he promptly handed to her.

Tasia opened it and read its affirmations of love. Near the bottom of the card, Kurt had written, "Tasia, do you love me?"

She looked away from the card and caught his eyes. "Yes, Kurt, I do love you."

Kurt smiled and reached for one of the crayons the waitress had left. Selecting the red one, he printed the words, "Will you marry me?"

Tasia picked up the crayon and scrawled, "Yes!"

He smiled broadly. His eyes were twinkling. Once more, Kurt reached into his pocket. This time, he presented her with a little box.

Tasia accepted the box, but before she opened it, she said, "Kurt, I also have some news to share with you." She recounted her walk in the woods earlier that day and her words of confirmation from the Lord.

Kurt didn't seem the least surprised by it. "You know, Tasia, I had a sense that if He was confirming it at my end, He would confirm it with you, as well." He looked at her with such caring – such love.

Tasia's eyes were getting moist as she opened the little box. Inside, resting on a field of black velvet lay the pear-shaped engagement ring she had admired weeks earlier at a jewelry shop. "Oh, Kurt," she looked into his shining eyes, "I do love you and will gladly be your wife."

He came around the table and took the ring out of its box. Reaching for her left hand, he placed the ring on her fourth finger and joyfully kissed her.

The waitress appeared shortly with their order and congratulatory wishes. A few other patrons turned around and clapped. Tasia blushed with pleasure.

As they continued on, waiting for their main course to be delivered, Tasia removed the ring from her right hand and tried placing it together with her engagement ring. "You know, what, Kurt? Take a look at this." Tasia held out her left hand. Her engagement stone fit perfectly within the setting of her 'God is faithful' ring – as if it had been made to order.

"Looks like a perfect fit!" exclaimed Kurt. He moved next to Tasia and put his arm around her. "Just like us."

Speak It Into Existence

by **Sesvalah**, LCSW
and **Naleighna Kai**

SPEAK IT INTO EXISTENCE

BY SESVALAH, LCSW

Every *word*, every *thought*, every *action*—controls the flow of your life.

Do you choose your words carefully? Does your life reflect exactly what you say? Do the words: "I'm broke," "I'm sick," or "I'm tired," sound familiar? What would happen in your life if you said: "I am prosperous" "I am experiencing an overabundance of energy," or "I am experiencing excellent health?"

Speak it into Existence expands on the belief that "If you change the way you *think*, you'll change the way you *live*."

The power of prayer, affirmations, positive spoken word, creative visualization, treasure maps, are fused with entertaining, humorous and heart warming examples and success stories of those who have used the Universal Principles to become entrepreneurs, buy home or cars, and heal from abusive situations and medical conditions.

If one sentence could change your life—what would you say? Think carefully before you . . . *Speak it into Existence.*

Speak it into Existence: ISBN: 0-9754130-3-1
Inspirational/New Age

SHE TOUCHED MY SOUL

Mykal "Magic" Arrington's sudden fame and startling climb up the music charts took his life into a downward spiral, ultimately separating him from his family and his hold on reality. Then he met Maya.

Unlike Mykal, who wishes to reunite with all that was once important to him, Maya doesn't want to deal with her past, even going so far as changing her identity. Mykal's newfound determination to get his life together could bring love and healing for them both, but may also cost Mykal his career . . . and Maya her life.

a novel by Naleighna Kai

Review taken from Amazon.com and BarnesandNoble.com:

What can you say about a book that has answered so many questions that you couldn't for most of your adult years? Is the word "Phenomenal" or could this book just be my inspiration?

She Touched My Soul" did exactly that in many different ways. The title grabbed me because I remember needing my "Soul Touched." The characters in this book are so real, the situations are believable….
As I write this review tears form in my eyes. I will never forget the characters in this book or the author who brought them to us.

--Missy, RawSistaz Reviewer

She Touched My Soul ISBN: 0-9754130-1-5/Fiction

The Things I Could Tell You! . . .
is the story of Cameron Spears, a Chicago teenager growing up in a house filled with secrets and domestic violence. After changing identities and moving to Memphis, the past comes back to haunt Cameron—forcing him to make a deadly choice that changes his life forever.

Acclaim for J. L. Woodson's
The Things I Could Tell You!

"*The Things I Could Tell You!* compels the reader to sit up and take notice."
    —Mary B. Morrison, national best selling author of
Soul Mates Dissipate

"I strongly encourage parents/adults to read this book because it shows what we, as women, tolerate sometimes for too long."
    —R. Hopes

"It's miraculous what J. L. Woodson has done at 17. I see the New York Times Best Seller List in his future."
    —Faye Childs, BlackBoard Bestsellers

"Writing with a finesse beyond his years, Woodson blends humor, reality and survival. He creates an inspiring story told with the innocent candor that can only exist when belief in humanity is still fresh."
    —RawSistaz Book Club

"This bright young author has written a story that hooks you in the prologue, which cleverly describes the intense ending of the story. The story is a pretty accurate portrayal of the effects abuse can have on a family and the extreme results that can occur. "
    —Darcina Garrett, The Literary Diversions Book

The Things I Could Tell You!: ISBN: 0-9754130-0-7

Fiction/Suspense

Colored Girls
Raised in the South

a novel by
Bettye Mason Odom

Beatrice Bush, from Vicksburg, Mississippi, on the cusp of becoming the first woman to create a multi-million dollar day spa empire, with the moral support of two other Colored girls raised in the south—Anna from Hunter, Alabama and Susie from Doolittle, Georgia.

These best friends tell a story that spans their lives from the time when Coloreds could not be served in public venues, to when Negroes began the civil rights movement, then when Blacks made a militant impact on politics, economics, hair, and fashion; and ending with the changes the three must make as modern African-American women.

Can they shake off the deep-rooted, southern-belle honor, obey, and stand by your man to find the happiness and success they cherish and deserve?

Colored Grits ISBN: 0-9754130-2-3/Fiction

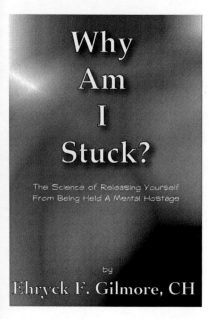

WHY AM I STUCK?

Are you your own worst enemy?
Why are you living with anxiety
and stress?

**Learn how you can have
an extraordinary life . . .**

o *Have harmonious relationships*
o *Live a prosperous life*
o *Enjoy perfect health!*
o *Have an exciting career*
o *Achieve lasting happiness*

Why Am I Stuck? is a guide to personal growth and positive
change in every aspect of your life.

Why Am I Stuck? inspires and motivates a whole new thought
process--the foundation to create the life that *you* desire.

Why are *you* stuck? Read this book and find out!

ISBN: 0-9754130-9-0/New Age/Metaphisical
author: Ehryck F. Gilmore, CH

A NOVEL BY W.L. WOODSON

Superwoman's Child: Son of a Single Mother by J. L. Woodson

Growing up the only male in a house full of women is no easy task. Sean's life has been filled with hilarious moments while trying to get away with anything and everything. But as he reaches high school, things turn a bit more serious and at times he wonders, will he make it to college? With his grades, will he even finish high school? If ever a he could use a male role model, now is that time.

Where is a good man when you need one? Especially since his father has been practically missing in action since he was two. How can Sean come to terms with the fact that the only people he needs in his life are the ones who actually love him, the ones who are already there?

Scheduled Release: June 2004
Superwoman's Child: ISBN: 0-97541130-8-2/Fiction

a novel by Joanne Fondren

Even inanimate objects have a life of their own!

Fiction/ISBN: 0-9702699-7-8

How to Win the Publishing Game

It's time to get out those old manuscripts and get them into print!

Avalon Betts-Gaston Esq. explains royalties and helps to avoid new author pitfalls;

J. L. Woodson teaches on the Redline Method of writing

Dr. Trevy A. McDonald helps you navigate their way through the self-publishing market'

Naleighna Kai explains what rejection letters are all about and what publishers are looking for;

If this book doesn't inspire you to get off your butt and write . . . nothing will!

How to Win the Publishing Game:
ISBN: 0-9754130-9-0, Self-Help/How To

Order your copy today!

MACRO PUBLISHING GROUP
Books/Novels for 2004

0-9754130-0-7	The Things I Could Tell You! by J. L. Woodson
0-9754130-1-5	She Touched My Soul by Naleighna Kai
0-9754130-2-3	Colored Grits by Bettye Mason Odom
0-9754130-3-1	Speak it into Existence by Sesvalah, LCSW
0-9754130-4-X	Touched by Love by Anne Freedman
0-9754130-5-8	Why Am I Stuck? by Ehryck F. Gilmore, CH
0-9754130-6-6	From Dry Places to High Places by Min. Earlee Hubbard
0-9754130-7-4	Trio by Naleighna Kai
0-9754130-8-2	Superwoman's Child by J. L. Woodson
0-9754130-9-0	How to Win the Publishing Game by Avalon Betts-Gaston, Esq.; Dr. Trevy A. McDonald
0-9702699-8-6	Bettye Odom: Face to Face by Bettye Odom, R.N.

All books are $14.95 except She Touched My Soul--$15.95

You can order novels/books from any leading or specialty bookstore; or receive autographed copies direct from the publisher: Indicate quantity, ISBN, and apply appropriate state tax.

Macro Publishing Group accepts money orders, cashier's checks (books ship out the same day of receipt). Personal checks may delay shipping by seven days. Make payments payable to *Macro Publishing Group* and send to:

Macro Publishing Group
Order Fulfillment
16781 Torrence, Suite 103
Lansing, IL 60438

For school, book club or bulk orders of 10 or more, call 888-854-8823 for discount pricing; or email: admin@macropublishing.com visit us on the web: www.macropublishing.com

Wife, mother, grandmother, speaker, educator, legal assistant and health aficionado are among the many talents of Anne Freedman. Born and raised in Chicago, Anne attended both private and public schools as a youth. She graduated magna cum laude from Northeastern Illinois University with a B. A. degree in Elementary Education.

Anne is a firm believer that one's body, soul and spirit are all intimately interconnected, and what affects one part affects the entire person and everyone around them. Her heart's desire is to make a difference in people's lives: physically, spiritually and emotionally. "Unconditional Love is what it's all about," Anne declares to those who are hurt, angry and disillusioned by the storms of life.

Anne now resides in Elgin, Illinois with her family and works for a leading law firm in the downtown Chicago area and is currently working on her next book.

annefreedman@macropublishing.com

888-854-8823